Soul of Love

By Joyce McCartney

Soul of Love, by Joyce McCartney

Copyright: 2016 by Joyce McCartney

Cover by Adam Brown

E-Book ISBN: 978-0-9863217-6-4

Print Book ISBN: 978-0-9863217-7-1

Available on Amazon.com

Table of Contents

Chapter 1:
The Shelter of a Home

The only thing Thelma could think to say as she listened to Claire's telephone call was "CRAP!"

Thelma Earnst and Claire Pike had been friends for a long time and called each other often. Thelma, a bit younger than Claire, was in her late fifties and, with her red hair and strong personality, delivered her opinion like a sharpshooter riding a wild horse. She lived in Cincinnati, Ohio with her granddaughter, Alexa, in the duplex Thelma had inherited from her parents and worked as a cook in a Jewish nursing home. Claire was in her mid sixties, her brunette hair now partially grey, and had been married to George for 26 years. The last year he had become depressed, then ill and recently died, a topic frequently discussed between the two friends. The current call was to announce that Claire had been forced to sell her home to pay debts.

"The first few months after he died, I cried all of the time, then I started to go through all of my husband's papers and found bills unpaid for a long time," revealed Claire, in a voice that shook with grief. "But it was the medical bills that shocked me the most. The nursing home bill was enormous. I refinanced

our home to try to pay them, but it still was not enough."
Thelma's four-lettered reply was brief and to the point, as it
usually was.

Thelma was an unusual person. As a child, she had been
able to hear from people departed from life. As an adult, she
occasionally did psychic readings for people wanting advice or
messages from their departed loved ones. For Thelma, a
reading meant looking upward at the ceiling, relaxing and
listening for the thoughts of whomever she wished to contact.
In fact, she had met Claire years ago when she had done a
reading for Claire from her mother and then later about
George's health. At that time, Thelma warned about the
worsening situation.

Claire recited the sequence of events. "For years, he'd been
horribly depressed, then they diagnosed him with cancer. The
last year, he'd been in a lot of pain and was being treated with
expensive drugs for cancer and depression in a nursing home.
Then one day, he just looked up at the ceiling and smiled saying
that he'd seen his parents, who had died. I knew then, he had
lost the will to live and he died later that week. After that, I felt
so lost and alone I could barely function and now I have all of
these bills to pay." Unable to fully accept the fact she was facing
building a whole new life alone, she talked on. "We had saved
for so many years so we could have a retirement, but having
refinanced the house to meet our expenses, there is no equity
left for me. I am alone and homeless."

Both women were evaluating the situation in silence and
then Claire continued. "On top of that, I've been diagnosed with
depression myself." Claire drew a breath, stunned to hear her
own description of her situation. She felt emotionally
overwhelmed and wept.

Thelma repeated her four-letter opinion. She was well known for being blunt, humorous and quirky, but, in fact, she only spoke the truth as she saw it. In her mind there was no point in avoiding the truth of any situation. But this time, after listening to Claire's description of her situation, Thelma thought for a long time, saying nothing. In fact, both women were silent for several minutes.

Thelma was sitting in her comfortable recliner in her upstairs/downstairs duplex in an old neighborhood of Cincinnati. The chair was simple, but functional. It provided some small comfort to Thelma's tired legs on bad days and was a great place to visit with friends on good days. Some fifty miles away, Claire also had sought comfort in her rocking chair. That's how they always talked, comfortably. As the silence served to settle the strong emotions, Thelma began thinking about her upstairs rooms being empty and her eleven-year-old granddaughter, Alexa, needing some supervision. And then there was the problem of Annabelle. Claire, on the other end of the conversation, was thinking about being homeless, alone and depressed.

"Thelma, I don't even know who I am anymore. I've lost everything and don't know what to do."

Thelma had been raised in the country, but later her family moved to Cincinnati where Thelma had taken care of her aged parents in their duplex home until they died. She then inherited the duplex where she now lived. Being a practical and feisty person who met the difficulties of life head on, she nevertheless had little to show for her life, but this house and her family.

In fact, her own life had not been easy. She had been married for a year in her twenties, when her husband made the almost fatal mistake of being unfaithful to her. Having discovered him out with another woman, although she was pregnant at the time, she literally threw him and all of his belongings out on the street. As she looked out the upstairs window at him picking up his clothes off the street below, she plotted how she would settle things her way, in her own time, and then some. As the last pair of jeans went sailing out of the window, she added her colorful insults for good measure. But then there was the unborn child.

Months passed and Thelma delivered a strong baby girl, naming her Annabelle. After some legal work, the attorneys and courts gave Thelma custody of her daughter, ceding her husband only visitation rights. Those visits, however, proved to be few and infrequent, leaving sad memories behind. Thelma raised her daughter, Annabelle, in the duplex as best she could, but the growing child had a mind of her own and rebelled against any and all common sense. In her teens, she began to buy and sell drugs. The two argued all of the time and finally in her twenties, Annabelle left in anger, slamming the door, only to be arrested a year later, pregnant with her own baby girl. After investigations with social services, Thelma took custody of her granddaughter, Alexa, and watched Annabelle go to prison.

Now at eleven years of age, Alexa needed more time and attention than neighborhood babysitters and Thelma's long work hours could give. But more to the point, Thelma dreaded the approaching day Annabelle would be released. Therefore, since the apartment upstairs had been empty for a long time, in Thelma's mind, there was something good that could come of all of this.

Finding her words, Thelma said to Claire, "OK, I've got a plan. Move in upstairs with me and help me take care of Alexa. We'll figure out the rest later."

There was a pause while Claire thought about the upstairs apartment being a retreat from a lonely and dangerous world.

Finally she replied, "OK, but don't expect too much from me. I'm not very good company these days. If you think you can put up with me, I'll list my house for sale as soon as I can and we'll see what happens. Thelma, what did I do to deserve this?"

"You did everything for him and nothing for yourself. Don't blame yourself, just get on stable ground and see what happens," said Thelma with uncharacteristic softness.

"God help me!" moaned Claire.

"He will," promised Thelma.

+

After many calls, the two friends had worked out the details of Claire moving into the upstairs apartment of the duplex. It was mid-March when Claire drove up to the humble house in a pickup truck borrowed from her brother, loaded to the sidewalls with her belongings. Thelma's house was in a working-class neighborhood with sidewalks good for mother's pushing strollers and children riding bikes. Most yards had small flower gardens and some even provided residents with vegetable patches now covered in snow. Thelma's yard had pink flamingoes stalking among her wild, tall grass, which would soon begin to send shoots from under the light snow. Thelma had little time to keep up with the wilderness that sprang up after every rain in the summer and her yard was known to be a home to misfit "volunteers" of many kinds.

In addition, Thelma's house was unique to the neighborhood in that it had a two-car garage and storage shed, thoughtful additions provided by her father. Inside the garage, there was plenty of room for a second car, if some boxes were to be moved around. In the shed, there was a bright new lawn mower and a movable Tiki bar complete with hula dolls, torches and a blowup swimming pool, all stored for Thelma's annual neighborhood summer luau party. Having a luau was not something her parents would have done, but it was definitely Thelma's style.

In addition, the duplex had a friendly and sociable front porch with a wide swing and some rocking chairs. Hanging from the porch roof were colorful, noisy wind chimes and empty bird feeders in bright colors bobbing in the wind. This is where Claire now stood knocking on the door, waiting for it to open. After a few minutes, she surmised Thelma and Alexa were not yet home, so she sat on the swing and tried to relax. She did not feel good at all. She had always been a bit depressed, even in childhood, but the current events added anxiety, tension, anger and a constant upset stomach to the mix, all of it capped off with negative thoughts about just about everything.

In her mind, even the pickup truck mocked her, giving evidence that, at her age, she should be happy and secure. At 63, how could she pack all of her belongings in a pickup truck? She had devoted her life to her husband and their life together, a fact leaving her impoverished emotionally and financially. What was she going to do about getting her own place? How would she ever be financially secure enough to retire? How would she ever have any confidence in herself again? Her parents would have been so disappointed in how her life turned out.

With such thoughts alive and well in her heart, even the family neighborhood seemed to point a finger at her suddenly single status, as if to say, *See you are alone. You have no one to care for you and never will again.* It was all a clear sign her life was in a shambles. Truthfully, she knew Thelma was right about not taking care of herself, so she blamed herself thinking, *What a failure I've been. I could have done better.*

She sat there watching the pink flamingoes bobbing in the wind in Thelma's front yard, innocently dancing with the wind in all of their pink happiness. Although they certainly didn't fit into a Midwest working-class neighborhood, there they were, living happily in a field of frozen weeds. Suddenly they suggested the promise that maybe she, too, could live there in peace, no matter how alone and out of place she felt. She relaxed into the swing and pushed it back and forth, taking her place among the oddities of Thelma's life. She started to enjoy the sunshine, the sound of birds, the racing of squirrels up and down tree trunks and the comings and goings of the neighborhood residents. It was a moment of calm and peace, much needed by her. *Yes, maybe I can get along here for a while until I think of something else. What other choice do I have?*

When Thelma and Alexa arrived, Claire gave them each a hug. "I am so glad to see you," greeted Thelma. "I see you got most of your things in the pickup truck." The comment caused sorrow to flicker across Claire's face and Alexa tried to soften the blow.

"Hi, Aunt Claire," said Alexa. "That your truck?" Claire's look of despair said "Not." They all paused in frustration and Claire sighed, releasing a few tears.

But even with such grief for herself, Claire loved her friends wholeheartedly and appreciated the offer of a place to live. And so they all carried her things up the stairs to place them in the little apartment to make it a home for her. With their help Claire turned her attention to converting the mostly empty rooms into a comfy place for her to retreat from life.

"Aunt Claire, do you want this table near the front window?" asked Alexa. "I think we can move the sofa over here, if you want."

"It is a nice window, isn't it? It feels like a treehouse view," noticed Claire. "Let's put the table and a chair there. That way, I can look out of the window and still read. That would be nice."

Claire wondered how she could possibly feel happy with all that was wrong with her life, but with such friendship, she did, just a little bit.

While Alexa finished helping with the move-in, Thelma descended the stairs and entered her kitchen, which was cheerfully styled in vintage 1950's, with Betty Boop salt and pepper shakers, turquoise blue tile on the floor and dancing dogs on her windowsill. Thelma surveyed her refrigerator and freezer, thinking about making supper. She had both full-sized units in her kitchen to hold all of the food she so loved to fix. Being a cook was her true calling, she knew. She found just the thing to serve for dinner in a package of frozen meatball sandwiches with a garlic topping. She put them in the oven to bake.

"Yum," she said to herself. " Now I just have to have my cola and a cigarette while we're waiting for that to bake." Even though the wind was cold, the sun was warm so she put on her coat and went out on her front porch for her time-honored ceremony of relaxation, smoking and chatting with the neighbors. Alexa and Claire were still hanging clothes in the closets and making the bed upstairs, but within the hour, they all assembled at the supper table for their golden brown sandwiches and the soon-to-be routine family talk at the dinner table.

"So tell me more about what happened," asked Thelma.

"I think I told you George had lost his job and retired on his Social Security three years ago, while I kept working. Then he got really depressed and just sat in his chair all day. He didn't look very well, so I took him to the doctor and they diagnosed him with cancer. He got much worse fast and the doctors said I wouldn't be able to take care of him at home. They recommended a nursing home and started giving him so many medicines, I couldn't keep track of them. I reduced my work to part-time hours so I could come to be with him, but he wasn't even conscious most of the time. Then the nursing home and doctors started sending me bills for what wasn't covered by insurance. I went to the bank and they suggested refinancing the house, so I did. That freed up a lot of money, but it all went fast to pay bills. Soon, I couldn't make the refinance payments," explained Claire. "Then he died."

"Why didn't you declare bankruptcy?" pried Thelma.

"I talked to an attorney, but she said I'd lose my house either way. She offered to try to negotiate a settlement for me," said Claire sadly.

"It's a heck of a situation. I would have sent him to hospice!" said Thelma.

Suddenly angry, Claire shot back "I didn't think he was going to die so soon! Well, maybe I just wasn't thinking very well at all. I wanted the best for him. Now, I'm stuck with it!"

Thelma was quiet for a moment and finally shrewdly observed, "You were always too unselfish, to a fault. You have to think of yourself. Nobody else will. It reminds me of my husband. I trusted him, but he was unfaithful and greedy." She paused, reviewing her own past tragedy. "Sometimes it pays to fight for what's yours."

Claire put down her sandwich, miserable and unable to eat any more.

Alexa felt sad for both Thelma and Claire, but thought of something hopeful in the words of a song she'd heard. She had thought about the lyrics a lot, wondering about their meaning. Now, she chimed in and said: " I heard a song that ended with the words, 'Who can tell what happens? When the time is right, then right is easy.'"

Both Thelma and Claire gasped and looked at Alexa, thinking the words were way too profound for an eleven-year-old to use. Maybe she didn't understand the meaning of the words, but she did know they might be helpful for the occasion. All pondered the words in silence.

The words to the song made Thelma think of something else that might help. "That makes me think of a book I bought at a garage sale last summer. I think I put it here with my cookbooks." She rifled among the old cookbooks with their ragged edges and handwritten recipes, to find a small book heavy with help. "Here it is. I've given it to several people, but they all gave it back to me saying they couldn't understand it. But I always thought it was full of profound truths. Maybe you could get some insights from it to help you," said Thelma, sliding the book across the table to Claire.

"Did you read it? Did you understand it?" Claire asked in annoyance.

"I read the first two pages. That was enough to know it said a lot more about life than anything else I *ever* read. You had some college, you'll understand it," rebutted Thelma with a wry smile. They both laughed, happy they could argue and still be friends.

Alexa left the table to check their email, something Thelma couldn't or maybe wouldn't do. Alexa did all of Thelma's Internet tasks for her, knowing she liked her independence from such things as email and phones. Actually, most people liked Thelma to stay just the way she was. She represented a courageous and honest heart, if ever there was one.

After dishes were done, the kitchen cleaned up and Thelma safely snuggled in her recliner in front of her favorite TV show, Claire took the little book and climbed the stairs for her first night in the duplex where friends intended to help each other.

The title of the book, which had only twenty-five pages, was *The Long Story*. Claire thought such a short book bragging to tell a long story couldn't be all that hard to understand. But before she could even open the book, her eyes became heavy and she relaxed into her bed. Quickly falling asleep, she dreamed of pink flamingoes and a neon sign blinking on and off saying "Who Needs the Grief?" The rest of the night was a void of darkness. In fact, Claire slept so deeply she did not even remember the dream when she awoke; however, the question would motivate her to change her way of life. And thus ended the first night of her fateful future in the little duplex. It was indeed a blinking neon future from which she would later emerge changed in so many ways as to make disaster seem fortuitous.

Chapter 2:
Who Wrote the Recipe for My Life?

The soon-to-be-very-familiar form of communication in the house was to yell up and down the stairs, which Alexa was doing early the next morning.

"Aunt Claire, Thelma went to work and I'm leaving to get on the bus. See you after school." Not hearing a response, Alexa left a note under the door for later, saying the same thing.

Rousing herself from the depths of sleep, Claire thought she'd heard something, but rolled over to dive back into rest and escape from her life. Later, when she finally awoke, she wondered how she'd slept so late, for a moment not remembering where she was and why.

Then Claire's eyes popped open. *Alexa? I have to get her ready for school. What time is it? Do I have to work today? What day is it?* She sat up in bed and then saw the note under the door. Thinking it not a good sign, she scrambled out of bed and rushed over to read it. *Oh no, I screwed up again*, she thought. Going into the bathroom to wash her face and brush her teeth, she looked in the mirror, where she saw herself, not quite herself. Her eyes were still blue and her face still slightly deformed on the right side as it had always been, but something had changed overnight. She was used to seeing herself as *The Victim*, but now she looked like *The Tired One*. She didn't think such self-observation was of much importance at the time, but she was later to learn that what she called oneself was very important.

Not ever having had a child of her own, Claire wondered what it would be like to care for Alexa and to be her fulltime honorary aunt. She also thought of herself at Alexa's age and realized how innocent a child is. *They know so little of what can happen to them. They think the world is a safe place.* Claire knew it was not. But, she thought she would enjoy taking care of Alexa and helping to give her a safe and happy childhood as best she could. Little did she know, it would be quite the reverse. Alexa had decided to take care of her as only an eleven-year-old can. Being a very unusual child with abilities and understanding well beyond her years, Alexa had inherited her grandmother's psychic abilities and truthfulness, although fortunately she had learned to voice the same in much more polite terms.

Finally, Claire located some jeans and a t-shirt, the old and soft ones that looked terrible, but felt good. *I missed my first assignment and I guess I'll be alone again today. Good thing, because I don't have the motivation to do much of anything,"* she admitted sadly. Seeing the day was unseasonably warm, a cup of coffee and the swing on the front porch seemed comforting to her.

Still in her comfortable slippers and a coat over her shoulders, she sat on the swing watching the families starting their days while the busy squirrels ran their routines through the trees. The sun was warm and soft as if it were filtering kindness through the branches, warming her arms and face. Slowly she started to think about the parts of her life she felt she could address, which in her current frame of mind wasn't much. For the rest, she felt that her losses were irretrievable and the grief and hopelessness too deep to even consider.

She decided, however, she did like baking bread and some years ago had taken some of her bread to a farmer's market in her former town to make a little extra money. The prospect of making bread felt familiar and easy, so she decided she would make a loaf of bread for the family supper tonight. It would represent getting back into some of her normal, comfortable routines. Stepping back into the 1950's, she looked through Thelma's very well equipped kitchen to assemble the ingredients. After mixing and kneading the dough, she returned to the porch with the little book Thelma had given her, thinking she would read it while the bread rose. But once again, she was overcome with sleep and, lying down on the generous swing, took a nap. Each time she woke to rework the dough she tried to read the book, but slept instead. Strangely she woke exactly when the bread was ready for the next step in the process and was glad she would have a successful loaf ready for her friends when they returned home for the evening.

Finally, she succeeded in opening the first page of the little book and read:

First there was God who is Love itself, living in peace.

Peace? Claire wondered. *I wish I had some of that!* She looked up just in time to see a bakery truck rumbling down the street with a design of a cake on the side with the words, *Have a piece of cake, it's easy.*

Easy? Claire thought. *Nothing in my life has been easy. My parents taught me to be a success, but nothing has worked out well. Now I'm alone and homeless, depressed and sick to my stomach all of the time. What does that say about God?*

At that moment her cell phone announced incoming email. It was her brother, Ernie, wanting to make arrangements to return her car and retrieve his truck. He also mentioned he had decided to change jobs. She replied with good wishes and a request he come with her to the final debt hearing if he could. Shortly the reply came, "Of course, you are my sister." Claire smiled in gratitude, remembering how they had always helped each other even as little children. She then thought of her deceased husband and the life they had made together, now gone. Ernie was now her only remaining family and she knew he would help and support her as much as he could. The thought of family made her feel better.

That reminded her to make an appointment to see the doctor again. The doctor had wanted to talk about her depression. Claire hoped Medicare would pay for it, as her part-time job doing bookkeeping at the dentist office and her Social Security didn't pay for much of anything. *I hate doing bookkeeping,* she sighed, recognizing another part of her life making her unhappy.

She returned to the house to call for her doctor's appointment, writing it down on the family calendar on the refrigerator and finally, feeling a little hungry, had some lunch. Refreshed, she wondered when the bus would come, bringing the children home from school. Putting the risen loaf into the oven to bake, she decided to sit on the porch all afternoon until the bus came. She picked up the book again to read the next few sentences.

God, being pure love, created a multitude of souls to love and a universe where they could live together in peace. The souls are God's children and existed within God and still do. They are the Beloved Ones, made from love, to be loved.

Claire turned the book over on the seat of the swing. *OK, you can just stop right there. I don't know who these souls are, but I'm not one of them. No wonder nobody wants to read this book. It talks about things that have no meaning to ordinary people. Who cares about these souls? Sorry God, I don't mean to be rude, but I don't see what this has to do with me. Good luck with all of the peace and love! I have problems to solve and I have to solve them by myself.* With that, the book was closed as tightly as her mind.

After the bread was fully baked, the bus arrived and Alexa and her friend Cassie descended with books, lunchboxes, sweaters and sneakers. *Thelma must have supplied all of that for Alexa*, Claire thought. *They truly love each other. Together, they are a family.*

Alexa waved goodbye to Cassie, who lived a few doors away and Cassie waved to Claire, calling her Aunt Claire with a smile. Alexa checked the mailbox and walked up to the porch, waving her most recent rental movie. "Look, Aunt Claire, my movie came. I can't wait to watch it."

Claire offered Alexa a piece of her bread and a glass of milk and they settled in at the kitchen table to discuss the day.

"I'm sorry I wasn't up to see you off. I just couldn't get up this morning," said Claire. "I'll do better tomorrow. What time do you get up to get ready for school?"

"I'm up at six and get my own breakfast. I can get to the bus by myself. How did your day go?"

"I made the bread, but it seems I slept most of the day. I'm really not very productive these days. I did start to read Thelma's book, but it didn't make much sense to me," said Claire.

"Let me see," said Alexa, pulling the book towards her and reading the first two paragraphs. "So what didn't make sense to you?"

Claire was startled to be asked the question by a child. She assumed Alexa wouldn't understand the book any better than she had, but she had underestimated the girl.

"The part about the souls and all of the love and peace. It didn't have much to do with my life. They are Beloved Ones! Who believes that?" summarized Claire.

"Don't you know you are a soul?" asked Alexa.

"What? No! What do you mean? What's a soul? Why am I asking you?" Claire scrambled for a way to stop this conversation.

Rebuffed by Claire's anger, Alexa grabbed her DVD and left for the living room to pop it into the player. Claire thought it would be a music and dance video or maybe a game, but she was wrong. The DVD was a documentary about archeological finds in Egypt. Repentant, Claire sat down on the floor beside Alexa in front of the TV and together they watched in blissful attention at the images of wall paintings in tombs and huge carved statues sitting outside of pillared temples.

"See, " Alexa said, "the Egyptians knew about their souls and built all of this. I just love archeology. I want to study it when I go to college."

Just then, the phone rang and Claire got up to answer it. Thelma called to remind Alexa of soccer practice. Cassie's mother was going to pick her up today and bring her home. Tomorrow, it would be Claire's day to ferry the pair to practice. Claire called to Alexa, who turned off the DVD and changed into her soccer clothes and shoes. When Cassie and her mother,

Diana, arrived, Claire introduced herself, promising to be the driver the next day and they left.

After that, Claire felt restless and decided to take a walk.

At the corner, she turned and headed toward the center of town, walking through blocks and blocks of very similar homes. She loved walking because it cleared her mind, gave her some exercise, but most importantly made her feel better. Near the town square, so prevalent in ethnic neighborhoods, she noticed a sign for an indoor farmer's market every Friday from 3 to 6 p.m. in the old arcade. She thought about how much she had enjoyed selling her bread at the market in her former town. She decided she could make some more bread and take it to sell in this new community, so she stopped in at the city offices to fill out the forms.

The man taking the application commented that she listed her product as homemade bread and asked her if she ever made rye bread. They conversed for a few minutes about rye, or rather he talked aloud about everything he knew about flour and bread making and she listened. In the end, he had misspelled her name on the permit and when she complained he said, "You can change that yourself. That will be $25." Again Claire complained and he replied, "Look, lady, do you want the permit or not?"

In the end, she had paid without having the error corrected. She left feeling not only rudely treated, but isolated and insecure. Sadly, she thought she didn't know who she was anymore, so maybe a name didn't matter after all. Hanging on the wall by the exit door was an army recruitment poster proposing, *Make Your Own Future, Join the New Army.*

When I was young, I thought I could make my own future, she thought to herself, *but everything has turned to dust. No, thank you for your empty promises, Uncle Sam, I think I'll just try to survive. Life's a burden and then you die.*

By the time she reached home, her feet and back hurt as well as her stomach, so she sat on the swing waiting for the girls to return and something better than her dire thoughts to happen.

At supper, the three talked about the day.

"How did soccer practice go?" Thelma asked Alexa.

"It's OK, we just do the exercises and chase the ball around, but it's fun," Alexa replied. "By the way, there's a school dance coming up soon. Can I go? Cassie wants to come, too."

"Of course. What fun! We should get you a new dress and Claire and I will volunteer for the dance committee," replied Thelma, winking at Claire.

"I don't wear dresses to parties anymore, Thelma!" objected Alexa as if it must be obvious that at eleven, the fashion rules change. "All I need is a good pair of jeans and a really great top."

"Oh, I see," smiled Thelma. "Well, then, we'll do that. I wanted to go to Goodwill some Saturday to shop for an outfit for the luau this summer. Want to go?"

"Sure, Cassie will, too. How about you Claire?"

"Yeah, I can use some jeans and t-shirts, I guess."

"So how did your day go?" Thelma asked Claire, suspicious the reply would not be good.

" I made a doctor's appointment to talk about depression and Ernie sent an email saying that he'd go with me to the final debt hearing. He said he's going to change jobs."

"Well, that doesn't sound so bad," challenged Thelma.

Finding her anger, Claire continued, "I went to the city offices to get a permit to sell my bread at the farmer's market and the man there was so rude. He misspelled my name and wouldn't fix it. He really didn't care if he did his job or even care who I was. It made me mad."

"You should have said, 'Do your job right, dude, or I'll report you to your supervisor,'" fired Thelma with one of her famous one-line confrontations.

"Yeah, I guess. People just don't care if they hurt other people. In the book you gave me, it says God made souls to be peaceful and loving, but look at what people do to each other. Look at all of the bad things that happen to people. What's that all about?"

"It's all about fear," said Thelma with a sigh. "I see it all of the time. People think they have to be pushy and mean to get what they want because they are convinced nobody loves them. He thought you were a pushover and he probably just wanted to take his break before the supervisor would notice. He just didn't care."

"Sounds like the theme of my life. I tried to do my best and I just get exhausted, alone and poor. Thank God for my brother Ernie and you two. You were good to me and took me in," said Claire thinking aloud. "Life doesn't make much sense to me anymore. Maybe I am depressed."

Thelma wanted to say, *You think?* but she actually said,

"How far have you gotten with the little book?"

"That's another thing. What it says doesn't make any sense either. It says God is love and all of the souls are supposed to live in peace. So where are they? I'd like to meet one of them and see how happy they are," complained Claire.

"Well, that brings us to the topic of Annabelle," Thelma wisely changed the subject. "I have to go to family visiting day at the prison on Sunday. Alexa, I don't want you to go this time. I have to work out some things with her and it won't be pretty. Claire, would you stay with Alexa for the day?"

"Sure! So what's going on?"

"She will be getting out of prison soon and we have to decide if she comes here to live with us," summarized Thelma.

"No!" said Alexa.

"No!" said Claire.

"I thought so, too" said Thelma. "So I found a halfway house for released inmates and I want to talk to her about going there."

"I hope that works out, but from what you've told me about her over the years, she won't do anything you say. She's one of those people who don't care if they hurt you," offered Claire.

"I know, but she's my daughter. I have to try. Thanks for the support," Thelma said pointedly.

For supper, Thelma had prepared a pot roast with corn and mashed potatoes, a classic country dinner from her childhood with her many siblings. "When I was a girl," she commented at the dinner table, " if a bowl of mashed potatoes or plate of meat was passed around, everyone would take as much as they could the first time it was passed, because it wouldn't come around again. It's the same at this table, only fewer people," she mused and helped herself to a huge spoonful of potatoes. They all laughed and pretended to grab the mashed potato bowl from each other. That was so much fun, Thelma started to scrape mashed potatoes from Claire's plate with her spoon. Claire grabbed her plate back. If Alexa had not said "Stop!" there would have been mashed potatoes flying through the air. Thelma was doubled over in laughter and didn't want to stop. While she was wiping her eyes, Alexa stole a slice of roast beef from her plate, but Thelma didn't even notice.

Later, on the porch, there was much more sensible conversation to be had among the three.

"So if people are mean out of fear, what is Annabelle afraid of?" Claire asked, wondering who could be more afraid than herself.

"She's afraid I was too hard on her because she's like her father. Maybe I was," said Thelma with a sigh. "We were both stubborn and afraid. Fear makes you do stupid things."

Claire thought about that for a while and then asked, "The book says God created souls who are peaceful and happy. Do you think you have a soul like that?"

"Do I look like I'm dead?" retorted Thelma laughing, then more seriously added "Yes, everybody has a soul. They are the spirits I hear from after people die. During life, a soul keeps us alive, guides us and continues on after the body dies. I never heard any of them complain, so they must have a good life wherever they are. What do you think, Alexa?"

Thelma and Claire leaned forward to listen closely to what she said as if a great wise guru were about to speak. Alexa began slowly and thoughtfully. "I think we *are* souls having a human lifetime. We all have a life plan that our souls help us with. Humans have just forgotten how to hear the thoughts of their own souls. It didn't used to be that way."

Now it was Claire's turn to demand an answer. "Just how do you know all of this? I never heard anything like that before."

Alexa shrugged her shoulders. "I just know it must be true. In my books, I see all of these ancient drawings and old artwork referring to spirits and they make sense to me."

"Actually hearing a soul's thoughts is a piece of cake," interjected Thelma.

"What?" Claire asked, remembering the truck with the image of a cake. "Give me an example!"

"While my mom was in jail," interrupted Alexa, " I was worried about what would happen to me, so I prayed about the plan for my life. I clearly heard, I'd live here with Thelma, go to college and become an archeologist. And that's what I am going to do. My mom's problems won't affect me. I'll be fine."

"How do you know you didn't make it all up because you wanted it to be that way?" Claire asked with a suspicious tone.

"It was good, so it had to be true and I didn't think it up, it just popped into my mind complete," Alexa said confidently. "It happens all of the time to everybody, they just don't believe it's really them talking to themselves. It's simple and easy."

"I always thought you had the ability to hear spirit," said Thelma, speaking to Claire. "Actually everyone has, it just depends on how much fear they have to block it all out."

"I can sometimes feel things, but I don't hear anything," admitted Claire.

In silence they pushed the swing back and forth for a while enjoying the early spring promise of warmer weather ahead, then Claire resumed with another question, while Thelma remained strangely quiet.

"What's a life plan?"

"A plan for your life is like a recipe for making bread. Everyone has one. Thelma taught me that. Didn't you know that?" queried Alexa, packing up her books to go to her room to do her homework.

After Alexa left, Thelma waited for a while and finally spoke. "I suppose you're wondering what your life plan is."

"Well, right now, my life looks pretty bad, so maybe I'd better not ask," said Claire. Then she added, "Who wrote the plan for my life?"

"You did and it looks pretty good to me from here on. You have reached a turning point. If you ever want to hear about your life plan, let me know. I'm going to bed. I'm whipped. Get it? Whipped potatoes?" She chuckled, or more precisely, cackled and left Claire on the porch to look at the moon and stars and wonder about the great mysteries of her life.

The moment was one of those later to sparkle in Claire's memory as being beautiful. The air was warm with the promise of spring and the breeze soft. The crickets were singing happy songs for the purpose of finding each other in the dark. The stars, the great wise ones in the sky, sparkled in the dark. Claire actually fell asleep on the swing and only later went up to bed, too sleepy to think of a thing. As she climbed the stairs, she saw a notebook on the top step, which Thelma had left out for her. On it was a Post-it note on which Thelma had written, *Take notes on the book. It'll help.*

Chapter 3:
Don't Be Afraid

The following Sunday morning, the little family rose with conflicting thoughts about Thelma's visit to the prison. After breakfast, Claire offered some suggestions.

"Tell her she would only be hurting herself by going back to a life of drugs and crime."

"She'd laugh at that, I suspect," said Thelma. "Then she'd say, 'What do you care, you never even liked me.'"

"So what are you planning to say?" asked Claire, noticing Alexa remained silent.

"I haven't quite decided, but I'm going to do a lot of praying on the way," retorted Thelma, putting on her jacket and picking up her keys. Alexa came over to her and gave her a big hug, saying, "I love you."

Thelma gave them both a kiss and a thank-you hug and went out to get into her car to leave. While she drove the hour and a half to the prison, she did pray in the only way that she ever found to be effective.

"God," she started, "I'll never know why you sent this angry child to me, but here I am with her. I know I can't let her hurt the three of us, or herself, but I have absolutely no idea of how to prevent it. Help us all."

Instantly, the very clear thought came into her head, *Just be there for her. We will send her to you in a new way.*

"Thank you, I will." In Thelma's mind, such succinct conversations were to be respected and honored, so she took a deep breath, relaxed and turned on the radio.

When she arrived at the prison family visiting room, she found Annabelle sitting behind a table with a face as belligerent as ever. "So what do you want today?" Annabelle was naturally blunt as was Thelma, and she typically used it to create ugly conflicts and to prevent anything constructive from happening.

"I want to talk to you about your release this summer," began Thelma.

"I'll bet you're sorry that I'm getting out, aren't you? You don't want to have to deal with me at all," challenged Annabelle.

Avoiding the obvious comeback retorts such as, *Why should I, the way you behave?* Thelma continued in a calm voice. "You have the option to spend some time in a half-way house for released women prison inmates. There you will have shelter, food and health care, but there are rules that you have to follow or they will turn you out."

"I can find my way around town. I don't need any shelter."

"And you cannot come to my house. I'm getting a restraining order so I can call the police on you if you do."

"That wouldn't stop me. Besides why would I want to spend any time with you? I have better things to do. Stay in your crummy house and do your pathetic job, I don't care."

"So, what else is going on here with you?" Thelma knew to change the subject.

"I'm so glad to be getting out of this god-forsaken place, I can taste it. Some of the other girls are jealous and some are giving me names to contact. It's all going just fine." Annabelle smiled in smug anticipation of a swift return to her old lifestyle.

Thelma lost her cool and foolishly tried to reason with her daughter. "Do you have any idea why you are so angry?"

"It's all because of you. You never loved me. You hated me just like you hated my dad, so don't pretend to be my mother. As far as I'm concerned, I don't have one. I'm bored with this conversation. I'm leaving, just go home." Annabelle got up in disgust and left.

Thelma got up as well and slowly walked through the prison passageways to the parking lot. There she looked up to the sky and prayed "God, we have to talk. I know I'm tough, but this is really bad. I'm afraid she will do us all harm and then die young. She is so afraid no one loves her, but I do love her. I love her so much. Help me!" With that she lit a cigarette and tried to relax. After a few moments, she heard the thought, *Do not be afraid.* With that, she recognized the answer she had requested and replied, *OK, then, you take care of it because I can't deal with it anymore.* She put her cigarette out and calmly got back into the car to drive home.

The drive home was filled with a jumble of thoughts. Thelma thought of her ill-fated marriage and how she and Steve had taken little time to really communicate about what they wanted in a marriage. She could only say they were young and married in a heated romance. She thought of the night Annabelle was conceived and remembered how Steve admitted he had been drinking and had taken some drugs. At that moment, Thelma began to fear for herself and the marriage. It was ironic Annabelle had been conceived at that moment, because it defined their relationship which never got any better. But she did raise her daughter with much love and hopes for a good future and was disappointed Annabelle came to have such a low self-esteem. In the end, she decided the ill-considered marriage had been a wild ride of an experience, but it was her ride and she did not reject it.

At the same time, Annabelle, sat in her cell, thinking about getting high when released. She remembered her first delicious high experience and how she craved to do it over and over again. Admittedly, she also remembered the painful feeling of withdrawal driving her to find another dose, sometimes several times a day. Between the ecstatic highs and the painful lows, she knew she was trapped in a world of dangerous crime and potential death with each dose. Knowing she was of low worth anyway, she knew a life of drugs was her proper place in life and she loved it. There was no reason to change.

Arriving home and getting out of the car, Thelma took a long deep breath of fresh air before coming into the house. There she found a note on the table saying Claire and Alexa had gone to the grocery store for some supplies to make a homemade pizza for dinner. Thelma gratefully used the time to take a warm bath and later to relax in her recliner.

When Claire and Alexa returned, they were surprised to see Thelma home so early and they both knew that things had not gone well.

"Thelma, you're home early. What happened?" Alexa asked.

"I said what I wanted to say and she said what she wanted to say and not much else," Thelma summarized. "Spirit says not to worry."

"Well, I'm glad you are home. It's early and we can still have a nice afternoon," proposed Claire optimistically. "What do you mean Spirit says not to worry?"

Both Alexa and Thelma sighed and looked hard at Claire, saying, "The souls, of course! They take care of problems if you ask right."

Then, Alexa changed the subject. "I have a report due for Ohio history and I wanted to go to Fort Ancient to see the museum there. They have a lot of artifacts of Native Americans who lived in Ohio."

"What a great idea!" Thelma replied, rising to the fun of an outing with her family. "Let's fix some sandwiches and have a picnic. Be sure to take your camera and notebook. Claire, get some directions and we'll be off!"

Thelma happily busied herself in the kitchen fixing a wonderful picnic. Soon they were driving away in her thrifty red car to visit the beautiful natural state park. Promising to be a happy event, they talked happily all of the way there.

At the museum they walked through the exhibits illustrating the ancient history of the area north of Cincinnati, learning about the geology of the land, the timber and animals of the forests and the little bands of still prehistoric tribes who raised their families, made their meals and clothed themselves from the bounty of nature.

"Look," said Alexa, " here's a sample of a dig the museum did to find the pottery and tools on display. That's what I want to do. I want to be the first to find something somebody made thousands of years ago. See that stone, it was used to grind grain. And that rock with a sharp edge was a knife to break open gourds and pumpkins. They used gourds for bowls and utensils. This is fascinating." As they walked through the displays depicting the history of the native tribes, Claire and Thelma smiled at each other to see the happiness the visit had brought to Alexa.

"Now we are seeing the influence of the white man," Alexa noted in her homemade tour. "They started out doing trades for food and hides, but later it turned to war. And look, here is a long canoe just like the Indians used for traveling the rivers. See the paintings on the side. I think they are prayers for the people who used the canoe. The Indians believed in a Great Spirit who gave them life and all that they needed to live."

On their way out of the museum, they selected some brochures Alexa could use for her report before asking for directions to a good picnic site. Sitting under very old oak trees, eating homemade sandwiches and drinking lemonade, they relaxed and chatted about living in Ohio, while Alexa's thoughts were much farther away.

"I wonder where I might travel to when I grow up," Alexa mused. "Maybe Egypt or South America."

"I hope not too far and wide, and don't forget the way home," smiled Thelma as she stretched out on a blanket for a nap. Alexa and Claire left for a walk on one of the trails branching out from the picnic site. Hearing the distinct call of birds that only live in such deep forests, they walked past spring wild flowers adding splashes of bright red and lavender to the drab leaf-littered ground. Time slowed down and Alexa's imagination ignited with an imaginary meeting with some Indians dressed in deerskin clothing coming down the trail, surprised to see them. Claire played along and they laughed, pretending to trade some jewelry for hides. It was a wonderful afternoon.

Later that evening over pizza and a salad, they talked further about the weeks ahead. Claire planned to practice her bread recipe and make it even better so she could sell it at the market. Alexa planned to finish her Ohio history report and go to the school dance with Cassie. Thelma planned to research the inmate halfway house further and to find out just when Annabelle would be released. With that they retired, each to their own room and thoughts.

For Claire, as night fell, she realized just how much becoming a part of this family pleased her and she hoped to always be there with them. She also hoped she could be of more help to Thelma and resolved to finish up with the debt hearing as soon as she could so she could begin to pay Thelma rent. Then sleep descended and her prayers for her little family were heard by the peaceful souls she had been reading about. Despite her skepticism, these spirits, the same Great Spirits the Indians had consulted, listened to her prayers with love and helpfulness.

Chapter 4:
I Just Want to Be Happy

The next morning, a bright sun shining through her bedroom window roused Claire out of bed, announcing a good day had arrived for her to see herself in a new way. She rose in time for an early morning breakfast conversation with Alexa. When the bus left for school, Claire returned to her apartment.

Her compact apartment consisted of three rooms. The bedroom just big enough for a bed, a desk and chair and a dresser, which Thelma had hand painted with colorful butterflies. The closet was small, but a wardrobe provided additional space for hanging clothes. Next was the spacious bathroom with a generous tub/shower, a toilet, a closet and two medicine cabinets. It was decorated with seashells, mermaids and antique crystal bowls filled with dried flower petals. The bright and clean bathroom was a pleasure to enter and use. This morning, as she looked once again in the mirror, she saw herself as *The One Better Than Yesterday*.

The only other room was a living room open to a galley kitchen and laundry closet. Unlike the ample downstairs kitchen, her kitchen was small, barely adequate and plain, but sufficient for Claire to prepare a simple meal. The living room, however, was generous, having a large window overlooking the front of the house. Instinctively, Claire had placed her rocker and a table and chair in front of the sunny window, an ideal spot to rest, think or read. The living room also contained a flowered chintz sofa, draped with her mother's afghan, faced by a coffee table. At the two ends of the sofa were end tables, which filled the corners made by the sofa and two small chairs. Not that it matched very well, but the furniture rested on a large burnt orange oriental rug, which declared the arrangement to be a sociable group of distinction. The rest of the apartment had well-worn wood floors with small rugs strategically placed to cover old flaws. All together the apartment was like living in a vacation cottage by the sea, cheerfully shabby, and somehow make-do and temporary. Best of all, it required little responsibility or upkeep, so it was a good place for the exhausted Claire to rest while recovering from the great disappointments of her life.

Claire knew she was less tired today than the day before, but the blue eyes and grey-brown hair framing her face in the mirror were still essentially portraying a sad picture. She was glad today was going to be busy. It was her turn to drive Cassie and Alexa to soccer practice after school, but before that, she wanted to perfect her bread recipe for the upcoming market. She dressed, again in old, feel-good clothes, mentally making a list of ingredients she'd need for her baking. She liked to make bread that was ornamental, so she used twisted shapes, which took a lot of flour. She would need to go to a good grocery store to find what she needed for the custom mix of flours she used to get the texture and taste she liked. Being oh so late already, she thought that she'd get a coffee at the grocery store. She hurried down the stairs, got into her reliable blue economy car and set off to the best grocery store in the area.

Upon returning home and unpacking her packages, she saved the receipt. She wanted to be sure that, in the end, she made more money than she spent. Her father had been of Scottish ancestry, therefore very frugal, and she was no different. She could not throw anything away until she had used it to its full extent and always compared prices and value before spending money on anything. When she worked on something, she thought about the most efficient way to go about her task. Her frugality gave her much satisfaction and through the difficult decline of her marriage, her good money management had helped her greatly to deal with the debts and to feel as if she'd some control over her life.

Then she thought about how her father had taught her to invest the money she had saved so she would have something of value when she was older. She knew by his standards, she should be better off by this stage of her life and she felt ashamed. Thinking about this, her energy sank and she felt tired and sick. Fortunately, her determination to make two loaves of bread, which she liked to do, saved her from a complete crash of hope.

She had always found the process of making bread very satisfying. It reminded her of her mother, a very good cook and housekeeper, who took the time to make homemade meals designed to be appealing and nutritious for Claire and her brother, Ernie. Frugality and homemaking, yes, these were inherited gifts from the values her parents had taught her and she intended to use them wisely. Suddenly, her energy returned and she conscientiously made her first braided loaf. It would be golden brown, crispy on the outside and soft on the inside. Yes, she thought to herself, *I am good at this!*

The rest of the morning consisted of the rising and kneading of several more loaves, leaving plenty of time for them to bake before Alexa would come home around three. While the dough rose, she sat down on the porch to rest and have a sandwich made from yesterday's bread. At times like this, when she was tired, she knew she needed to drink a lot more water. Sometimes, she realized she felt bad just because she was thirsty and she had recently become aware how she purposely ignored the need to drink water when she was depressed. Having gotten very sick as a result on several occasions, she now got up, filled a large glass of water and drank it all. If her mother were there, she would say, "Claire, take better care of yourself. You are a beautiful and competent woman and I love you." Bringing tears to her eyes, the memory attested to how she still missed her mother, now deceased twenty-one years. Her parents had valued her as she was and looked after her in a kind way. In fact, she hadn't been loved like that since her parents died, not even by her husband who needed more support than he gave. She even wondered if she had really loved her husband enough and he her. Sighing, she hoped her parents weren't disappointed in her being homeless and alone. More importantly, she was disappointed in herself and how her life had turned out.

I can't think these thoughts, she lectured herself. *They make me too sad.* She got up, cleaned the kitchen and was wrapping the finished loaves of bread by the time Alexa arrived.

The trip to the soccer practice and back was a refreshing look at the lives of the local school children and their parents. Claire resolved to remember all of the names of Alexa's friends and their families and, of course, the score of each match, despite the fact that Alexa regarded the game as mere exercise and fun, having no true passion for winning. The evening supper was pleasant and reassuring, despite Thelma's description of all the confusing things people can do to screw up a deli department in a Jewish nursing home. In blending their lives together, Claire felt the three of them were forming a family, each helping the others to succeed with her own goals.

+

The day of her first farmer's market, Claire rose early enough to see Alexa off to the school bus after having provided her with a breakfast of oatmeal and applesauce, much like her own mother always did for her. Then she packaged her bread so as to be ready for the market that afternoon. She loaded her car with a folding table, bags and a change tray, thinking selling bread was really a simple thing. People love farmer's markets and come from all around for the fresh, unique foods, such as her bread. Labeling the loaves by flavor and design, she was proud of her bread and knew the loaves would easily sell. Having arranged for Alexa to stay with Cassie and her mother after school until she returned, she felt ready for her day.

After arriving at the market, she quickly set up her table and chatted with the other vendors. A man who had a dairy farm was setting up a table of homemade yogurt, butter and whole milk, which was pasteurized, but not homogenized, as he declared. Vegetable farmers had set up tables loaded with hothouse lettuce, baby spinach, dried garlic and chives. Claire walked by each box of vegetables thinking of the good meals they would make. Looking forward to spring as it offered the first beginnings of the delicious plenty a garden can produce, she also knew summer and fall would yield pumpkins, potatoes and apples, all the goodness of gardening.

A young woman who made homemade soaps and scented bags of flower petals was also setting up. Beside her was an Amish couple, selling eggs and a variety of baked pies, donuts and cakes. Thinking the three living in the duplex could have eggs and toast before the shopping trip to Goodwill on Saturday morning, Claire bought two dozen of the fresh, large, brown Amish eggs for a reasonable price.

At her own table, Claire's bread was selling fast, when a round, short German man stopped by her booth and asked if she made pretzels. Before she could answer, he started talking about pretzels and how he makes them at home. He went on and on, giving her no opportunity to say a thing.

Just like a selfish man to spout off about himself, and not listen to anyone else, she thought. He continued to talk while she packed up her last things. She even started to walk away from the man, but he kept on talking. She wondered how long it would take before he realized he was alone.

Suddenly, he asked, "Why did she leave me?" then continued his monologue about pretzels. Claire heard the question, and nothing else. Apparently unaware of having even voiced the heartfelt question, he eventually wandered down the row of tables to talk to the other vendors in much the same manner as he had to her. She suddenly felt very sad. Sad he was so lonely and sad she couldn't answer the questions for herself, *Why did my husband have to die? Who will love me now?*

Arriving home, Claire sat on her chintz sofa and counted her proceeds from the sale of her bread, comparing her sales against her expenses. She was satisfied she had made about $30, which wasn't a lot of money, but it was much needed.

The question from the man who talked about pretzels petulantly intruded into her thoughts. Picking up the notebook Thelma had given her and writing the questions, "Why did my husband have to die? Why am I alone? Who will love me?" she was glad the questions were on paper and no longer just in her mind. They were very toxic questions and she never arrived at any good conclusion when she pursued the answers. She decided to open the book about *The Long Story* once again, planning to read a little farther than she had before. But first, she reread the part about how all souls are Beloved Ones, created to be loved.

Suddenly angry at her own situation, she picked up the book, walked to the staircase and threw the book down the stairs. Upset and tired, she stretched out on the sofa to take a nap, refusing to think or feel the impact of the questions she had written in her notebook.

She slept until Thelma, who had picked up Alexa, came home and started supper downstairs. Thelma found the eggs in her refrigerator and was glad to have them. She considered making waffles for dinner, provided she could find some good sausage to go with them in the freezer. *Yes, she did! What good fortune*, she chuckled, as she started to prepare the waffle batter. In time, she wondered what was going on with Claire. Starting up the stairs, she found the book lying open on the stairs. *Uh, oh,* she thought to herself. She finished climbing the stairs, knocked on the door and found Claire sleeping on the sofa. She sat down beside her in the end chair and read the questions in the notebook. Shaking Claire out of her sleep, she asked, "Do you want to talk about it?"

"No, I don't," replied Claire. "There's no good answer to those questions."

"OK, supper will be ready in a half hour. Clean up and come down. Here's the book back. Keep reading it. It'll eventually make some sense." Claire refused to even look at it.

At supper, the three worked their way through a huge pile of brown and crispy waffles and a plate of juicy sausages. It would take more than the three friends to consume all the food, but it was the generosity that counted.

"There were a few fresh green early vegetables at the farmer's market today. Do you want me to bring some home next time?" Claire asked.

"As soon as they have fresh spinach, get some of that," ordered Thelma. "Later in the summer, I'd love some green beans and Silver Queen corn." Thelma was enjoying her third waffle and asked about Alexa's day, trying to avoid asking Claire the same question.

"Cassie and I want to look for some new t-shirts. Can Cassie go with us to the Goodwill store tomorrow?" said Alexa.

"Of course, just ask her mother. It'll be a blast," said Thelma. "We'll leave about 10. Claire bought some country eggs, so I thought we'd have eggs and toast before we leave. What do you think?"

"That is exactly what I was thinking, when I saw the eggs at the market," said Claire. "Are you reading my mind?"

"Can't say as I'd want to today," replied Thelma, turning to confront the inevitable head on. "Do you want to talk about whatever is bothering you so much?"

"OK, OK. So why does the book say all souls are Beloved Ones, when bad things happen to people? People do such mean and selfish things to each other! Furthermore, most people have no idea how to love somebody. Today at the market, there was a man who talked, but wouldn't let anyone else talk. He didn't even know I was there. How selfish is that?"

"He's not selfish. He's afraid," said Thelma, patiently revisiting her prior comments on the matter while lighting her cigarette. "Fear accounts for most grief on the earth today. That's my opinion."

"Afraid of what?" inquired Claire.

"Afraid he isn't loved. Just like you. Everybody's the same," said Thelma, her eyes focused on the ceiling, following the smoke from her cigarette curling upward, like when she does psychic readings for people.

Claire considered Thelma's words and said, "He came to my booth and I would have talked to him, but he wouldn't let me. If he wanted to be friendly, why did he fake friendliness and at the same time drive people away? He really made me mad!"

Furthering her own thought, Thelma added, "After a long time of believing he is alone, he has made it his life. He thinks if he doesn't try to make a friend, he won't be disappointed. It's a case of cold, dry fear, stubbornly entrenched. His mind is closed and may never open up to something better," prophesized Thelma with unaccustomed wordiness.

"I'm glad you aren't like that, Aunt Claire," said Alexa. " If you were, you'd get old and sick fast.

"I am old and sick," retorted Claire.

"You can change that if you want to." Thelma charged back into the discussion. "Don't you want to be happy?"

"Sure, everyone does, but after so much evidence to the contrary, I've given up hope," pouted Claire.

"See, that's what the man at the farmer's market did. He gave up and is living behind his defenses. That's not the way you will end up, my friend. Face the facts. Your marriage is ended and you have to start over again. Now you can choose something different. Get over it and get on with your life." Claire and Alexa were not shocked at Thelma's blunt statements. It was her way of loving her friends and family.

"It's Friday, let's watch a movie tonight. There's a funny movie about a family vacation that goes crazy. I love those kinds of movies," offered Thelma.

"I'm tired. I think I'll take a walk and then go to bed. I'll feel better tomorrow," countered Claire.

"Suit yourself," said Thelma. "Alexa, are you in?"

"Yeah!"

As Claire walked the neighborhood, she saw some homes with families and some that appeared to have people living alone. Thinking of widows and widowers she knew, she wondered how many of those marriages had been happy ones and how the people left behind made new lives for themselves living alone. She wondered if they ever felt loved. *In fact, how many people in general feel loved at any point in their life? Damn few, I'll bet. In fact, what was love after all?* Her face got hot with the question, but no answer came. The moon cleared its way from behind some clouds, flooding the sky with white light and flashing some of it across the sidewalk for her to see her way. The night crickets and frogs serenaded their unique versions of family life and finally, the walking calmed her down.

When she returned, she could hear the movie playing loudly in Thelma's living room accompanied by laughter, but she ignored it and climbed the stairs to her own place. There, she opened the notebook and crossed out the question "Why did my husband have to die?" and wrote, "I just want to be happy."

Although she had earlier taken a nap, she readied for bed and quickly fell asleep. The moon and stars kept watch over her through her bedroom window, showering her with the same quiet white light she saw on her walk. She had no way of knowing it at the time, but great things come from small changes such as she had made this day in her notebook. In fact, the most fateful thing she ever would do was to write the simple statement "I just want to be happy." She would soon find she had awakened the proverbial genie in the bottle.

Chapter 5:
Good Grief

Sometimes when a person sleeps very deeply, there is a feeling of completely letting go of everything that constitutes familiar everyday life. When Claire awoke the day of the great shopping trip to Goodwill, she felt completely different than the day before. She recalled a series of dreams from the night that were humorous and perplexing. She had dreamed of a pig in her bathroom taking a shower. Then came a dream about a beaver with two tails who decided to bite one off. Finally, she dreamed of three bears shaking trees to get the bark off, but then walking away, left the bark to blow away in the wind. How weird was that?

Because it was Saturday, she did not have to get up as early. While she was still in bed, she sat up and recorded the dreams in her notebook. No sooner had she done that, then she heard the two housemates downstairs working in the kitchen. She hurriedly dressed and went downstairs to a true country breakfast of fried eggs, biscuits and gravy and toast, complete with hot coffee and Danish from the local bakery. It was easy to see Thelma loved cooking, but hard to see how she stayed so thin. Seated at the generous breakfast table, Claire talked about her dreams.

"Anybody have an idea of what the dreams mean?" Claire asked. This morning she was hungry and talked between bites.

"Time to cast off the old and put on the new," proposed Thelma with her mouth half full. She really didn't want to talk when she was enjoying her food.

Alexa was more thoughtful because she considered dreams to be very interesting. She pulled out a book on dream interpretation from the cookbook shelf, where all of the good books were kept, and carefully looked up the symbols relating to the pig showering, the beaver biting off a tail and the bears shaking bark off trees. After reading from the book, she summarized, "I think the pig taking a shower means that you are 'going through a period of cleansing.' And the beaver with two tails is the 'end of one reason for living and the beginning of another.' The bears are those who are helping you 'peel off grief so you can be happy'."

"Wow," said Thelma, "that's a pretty good interpretation. Did I buy that book? I'll have to use it more often. Do you think it fits you, Claire?"

"I guess so. But I don't get why a period of cleansing is so important. So I get rid of some bad feelings and memories. How does that help me?" Claire wondered aloud. Thelma looked at her with an expression of *Get real, honey*, but actually said, "Let's get the kitchen cleaned up. I hear a shopping trip calling me. Last one in the car buys the gas!"

To say they had fun at the huge Goodwill store was an understatement. To say they got bargains was a truism. To say only half of the prized garments would ever be worn and the rest most likely be returned to the same charity, was a certainty. True to expectations, Thelma bought a frilly satin dress with a tropical flower print and a plunging back. She thought it would be perfect for the luau she would host this summer. Alexa and Cassie each bought bright t-shirts painted with fantasy designs and a few sequins. The tops would go with their *Oh, so tight* jeans that were most certainly not meant to attract a boy's attention, but probably would. Claire found a sturdy new apron, a pair of jeans, a sweater and three t-shirts. With what she already had, they represented enough clothes, she thought, to keep her going for at least a year or more, all for $20.

The drive home was full of happy talk. After they unpacked the car, Claire went to the mailbox and found the first piece of mail for her at her new address. It was from the dentist office where she worked part-time doing bookkeeping. She opened it carefully, wondering why they had sent her a letter rather than talking to her this week when she came into work. She scanned the letter to see that it was, incredulously, a letter of termination of her job. It said she had been laid off due to cost cuts at the office. Once again, Thelma contributed her four-lettered opinion. Claire was stunned, her hands shaking. Alexa was thoughtful. All were thinking that once again something bad had happened to Claire . . . or maybe not.

"You hated that job. I'll bet the job ended because something better is coming along," mused Thelma. "It's like in the dreams."

"Ditto," supported Alexa.

"What else bad can happen to me?" Claire said through tears. "I'm tired. I think I'll take a nap." It had been a happy day and needed no clouds to show up in her life, but they did. The termination brought an uncertainty accompanied by the possibility of more bad things yet to come. Only sleep could offer comfort, even if only temporarily so.

Upstairs, Claire lay down on her sofa and covered herself with the afghan her mother had made for her and quickly fell asleep. It was a thoughtless sleep which completely rearranged her view of her world. After an hour's nap, Claire woke and surprisingly was less depressed about the loss of the job. She realized she hated the job, not because of the work or the people, but because it was hard for her to concentrate on bookkeeping, considering her mental state. Probably, if truth be told, and it certainly would be if you asked Thelma, Claire hadn't been doing a very good job of bookkeeping since her husband had died. In addition, it was a long drive to the office now that Claire had moved to the duplex. Without the job, at least Claire would have more time to help Thelma, begin to think about starting over and, of course, bake bread. She began to form a strategy based on the tried and true lessons of industrious frugality her father had taught her in childhood.

She calculated that if she tripled her bread production each week, she could make up for some of the lost income and she wouldn't have the expense of driving to the office. She could begin to pay Thelma some rent and draw a little from her small savings to make ends meet. But the bread would have to be good, very good. With this goal in mind, she began to think about new and better ways to make her bread more appealing and profitable. Before long, she was in her kitchen assembling her bowels, spoons and flour to try out a variation on her favorite bread recipe. She wanted a sample to be ready by supper, so Thelma and Alexa could critique it. She carefully organized her ingredients, wanting to completely enjoy the process, one of the few things left in her life to enjoy, she mused. She was not even aware of time passing while she was baking. Most importantly, she even forgot to feel sad.

She consulted her best recipe, evaluating it carefully. Assessing what she could improve, she decided the basic recipe was so reliable she didn't want to change it. But she did want something special about the bread. She waited for a good idea to form. When it did, it truly delighted her. The thought suggested she could add some herbs for flavor and color. She wondered which herbs would be best, for she had many. When the clear thought of rosemary and dill came to her attention, it wouldn't leave, so she took the two herbs down from the cupboard and opening them up, smelled their aroma. Without doubt, the blending of the two would be very nice, but just how much of each? Clear as a bell, she thought one part rosemary and two parts dill would be perfect because dill was a delicate taste, but rosemary could be quite strong. With that in mind, she began her recipe with great pleasure, planning to add the two herbs at the end of the mixing.

Before she finished the mixing, however, she stopped and seemed to be frozen in thought. This special bread needed something else. She stood alert, waiting for another great idea to fall into her mind. There it was! Add orange zest! She habitually shaved and dried some orange and lemon peel whenever she had those fruits available and kept the dried peel in glass jars on her shelf. Drying intensified the flavor and made the peel crispy. She took two pinches of orange zest and crumpled them in her hand, rubbing them until the aroma was released. She was delighted to know the smell was strong and seemed a good match to the herbs. Then she sprinkled the orange peel crumbs and herbs into the dough and finished working it. Yes, this would be wonderful! She would let it rise and finish baking it by suppertime.

Satisfied, she sat down at the desk and pulled out her notebook and the little book, *The Long Story*. In the notebook, she wrote: "Lost my job today, but I'm glad. I'm baking bread with rosemary, dill and orange peel to sell. Why am I so happy about that?" She then opened the little book that was so hard to understand, noting she was only on the first two paragraphs of page one. She read the next section.

God and the Souls lived in spirit form for eons of time in perfect happiness when God decided to create a physical universe in which they could give birth to new minds. With that thought, all of the galaxies, stars, planets and moons began to form, all within the body of God.

Upon the earth, the souls took the life, over which God gave them care, and developed life from simple cells to more complex animals and finally, humans.

In evolving humans, a nervous system and brain was developed which housed the developing human minds. These human minds were free to choose between fear and love.

But there was a second nervous system which the soul mind used exclusively to keep the human body healthy and happy. The soul of each human surrounded the body in the form of a light-filled aura, helping mankind to prosper.

And so, humans essentially have two minds, the human mind and the parent soul mind. At times these two minds were peacefully in cooperative contact and great civilizations were formed. When there was no contact, humans felt alone and afraid, forgetting who they were and war and poverty followed.

Claire closed the book and checked her bread, muttering to herself, *Two minds? No wonder I feel like I'm crazy most of the time.* And a little while later, she thought, *Alone and afraid! Tell me about it!*

During the rising process, bread is very aromatic and Claire had learned to judge the progress of the bread from the smell. Raising the cloth over the bowels to both see and smell the dough's golden goodness was just too satisfying to skip. As it was time to punch the dough down for the second rising, she thought of her dream of the bears shaking the trees. She wondered why they wanted the bark off when it was just going to be carried away in the wind. Suddenly she thought of the man who talked about pretzels. To save himself from his fear of not being loved, he had protected himself from any meaningful interaction with a potential friend by never letting anyone talk. He did this because he was afraid. He had essentially grown protective bark, which kept him from being hurt. That seemed to give her the answer to her question as to why fears had to be eliminated. People who have strong fears build up defenses, which keep them from getting what they truly want and need to be happy. Just what Thelma had said! It was a conclusion worth writing in her notebook.

After the bread had been kneaded, she returned it to the safety of its warm bowel, covering it with a damp cloth. She returned to the desk and wrote in her notebook.

"Don't hang on to fears, they make it harder for you to be happy. I don't want to be fearful, I want to be happy." She was about to put the pencil down when she thought how happy the idea for the herb bread made her feel. Making bread was already a happy thing for her to do, but it had also helped her to see a way to earn some money. In fact, the thought that she was helpless to change her fate in life was an old fear that had always sent her into depression. The bread idea proved that thought untrue. In fact, changing her fate had been easy and delightful to accomplish. Furthermore, she remembered with delight she had the ability to get really good ideas when she needed them.

Once again, she stood up to leave the desk and get a glass of water when the thought came to her loud and clear and would not leave. *If I can triple my bread production, I can prosper as much as I want.* Being such a good and wise thought, she had to write it down as well. She wrote, *The great bread idea gave me hope that I could make a living all by myself doing something I love. Because of the great idea for my bread, I can make a new life for myself.* She put the pen down with pride. She felt happy she had captured such a great thought on paper, where it would never be forgotten. She suddenly remembered why she had always loved to write.

Yes, that is what I will tell myself whenever I think the sad thoughts, she decided. Seeing the day was still bright and she had a half an hour to spare, she decided to take a walk. In fact, she felt she could walk for hours and never get tired, quite the opposite of how she had felt for months and certainly how she initially reacted when she got the notice of termination. She had faced a fear, found some hope and felt much better. It was good to be without fear. She realized fears had a lot to do with her stomachaches.

Checking her rising bread one more time, just because she liked to do it, she prepared to go outside for a short walk around the block. But then, she stopped in her steps. Her feet were frozen with a question so profound it would change her life and those around her. *Who gave me the idea for the bread? Who gave me this hope? I asked a question and I got an answer, a great answer, and it wasn't me, I know that.*

She returned to the page in the little book, which talked about the two minds and suddenly she understood something she had always known, but never realized was so important. Indeed, the idea for the herbs in the bread was in the category of something given to her, not something she thought out for herself. She had heard from her other mind, her soul mind.

She went back to the desk, picked up her pen and wrote the question that was going to change her life, *Who am I communicating with?* She paused to wait with attention for the answer, just as she did with the ideas for making bread. Quickly, it came to her mind, *We are thinking this together, you and I. We are one and the same, sharing this lifetime.*

Claire dropped her pen, got up and quickly walked to the other side of the room as if to avoid someone. She was drawing deep breaths in confusion about the moment, when she suddenly laughed, realizing it was only herself, her Soul Self, so to speak. Startled, at first, to get an answer so clearly from some other source, but recognizing its beauty, she wrote the thought down word for word and compared the question to the answer and the paragraph in the book. Yes, something very profound had just happened. Deciding the dialogue was not a bad thing, but most certainly a good thing, she was not afraid, but rather intrigued. Suddenly, she didn't feel so alone anymore.

With that, she became aware that more time had passed than she had thought and the bread was ready for baking. Placing the bread in the hot oven, she felt she now needed a walk. Setting the timer on her cell phone, she left for a walk around the neighborhood with the happiness of a grand thought in her heart. *I am not alone! Maybe I have help. I am not little and helpless.*

And indeed she was not. Returning, she found the most wonderful loaf of bread she had ever made waiting for her to remove from the oven. Nearing suppertime, she wrapped it up in a towel and took the hot loaf downstairs to the kitchen for the family supper. There, she found Thelma, who was thinking about what to fix for supper.

"What do you have there?" Thelma asked. "Yum, smells good. That would go with chicken stew," said Thelma, opening her refrigerator door. "Want to help?"

"Yes, of course. Thelma, I have to tell you, this is the best bread I've ever made. I want to make a lot to take to the farmer's market next week to sell. I don't care about losing the bookkeeping job. I like making bread far better than doing bookkeeping. Want me to chop vegetables?"

Claire continued as she chopped carrots, celery and three potatoes. "I had the most amazing experience while I was making bread today. I was thinking of ways to make my bread better and ideas about using herbs popped into my head. I know I was not making it up and the ideas were wonderful. If I asked a question, the answers came to me. It was like someone was talking to me and I could know their thoughts. I started writing them in the notebook. Has that ever happened to you?"

"Yes! That's how I do psychic readings," confirmed Thelma. "I think of a question and wait until the answer comes into my mind."

"That's exactly what it was like for me. I just waited, like I was waiting for someone to answer the phone and start talking to me. It was amazing, the ideas were great and it felt so good," said Claire. "And there is a certain happy feeling that comes with it, right?"

"Yeah. That's how I know I got it right. If it makes me feel good, then it's right. If it's scary, negative or iffy, it's not right," continued Thelma, placing the vegetables in a soup pot with some chicken. "It's always been that way for me. I was eight before I realized not all people do it. Nowadays, people think being psychic is a great mystery or spiritual power, but to me it's just normal."

"How do you know it's not something you wanted to make up?"

"The answer is always good, well, really better than good. I mean it is something I would not ordinarily think and it solves a problem or gives more help than I expected. It's never scary, negative or judgmental. I recognize it when it's right. Oh, I don't know how to describe it. You are better with words than I am."

"And it feels like somebody loves you," finished Claire. "I think I've been doing it all of my life, but I just never realized what it was. The book says it's my other mind, my soul mind."

"That's a good way to describe it. And, you know, souls talk to souls. They are a big family and know each other very well. That's how I get answers from people who have passed over. I call it Spirit or God, but they've always been there for me and never let me down," said Thelma.

All of the sudden, laughing, Claire said "It's sort of like a big communication that's always going on. Like a social media website. . . You just have to log in and start a conversation. The little book says people have these two minds, but sometimes the human mind doesn't know the soul mind and they live in fear."

"Oh, I agree with that. And once you're in fear, you can't hear your soul. I have to be in a certain frame of mind to be able to do a reading. The whole thing has to be kind, peaceful and loving. Fear would certainly make it impossible. So what else happened?" asked Thelma.

"Well, I decided to write questions in my notebook and then write down the answers I got. I asked who I was communicating with and the answer was, 'We are thinking this together, you and I. We are one and the same, sharing this lifetime.' What do you think of that?" Claire asked.

Thelma stopped cooking for a moment, saying, "The soul mind is smarter and wiser than us, so we should ask a lot of questions about life and our problems. It's a lot easier than trying to figure things out by ourselves. Remember what Alexa says about archeology and old civilizations?"

Claire resumed the meal preparation, realizing ancient people knew the soul mind was more powerful than they and could help them. They called them gods, but the people knew how to communicate with them for good results. How did modern society get so far away from such a simple source of help?

The three gathered for supper and continued their discussion over chicken soup and rosemary bread, a delicious meal celebrating a wonderful day.

Claire teased Thelma, "So which god did you pray to for making chicken stew?"

"Not the chicken god," quipped Thelma with a laugh.

Alexa pried Claire with the question, "Well, then who is the god of making bread?"

"You better say goddess. I think I remember the Greek goddess of grain is Ceres from whom we get the word cereal."

"Well, the only god that I'll ever make sacrificial offerings to is the god of chocolate," said Thelma. "Now that was a really good gift to woman kind." They all laughed. It was a conversation few homes in the area would consider normal, but the little family didn't care. They felt happy and wanted to celebrate.

Rising from the table, Thelma summarized it all by saying Claire losing her job had been *good grief*. They all smiled in agreement and Thelma went to her chair to enjoy the evening's TV shows. Claire offered to clean up the kitchen and Alexa went to her room to read her books. Later, Claire returned to her room to write in her notebook. Each did so with a last slice of rosemary bread spread with butter and jelly for dessert.

Once the genie had been let out of the bottle, so to speak, there was no getting it back in. Being peaceful and asking for help was like saying *Open Sesame* and seeing the doorway reveal mysterious and benign parts of oneself. And so Claire wrote in her notebook that night and many more to come. She wrote about her depression and her grief, her fears and hopes, but also about new recipes for bread and how to help her friends. After all, it was her own soul mind giving help with her own problems and she could ask whatever she wanted. Most importantly, she was not alone.

Chapter 6:
No Doubt

When one has been standing for a long time on the bridge of life looking down at the murky water below seeing nothing but gloom, and a ray of sunlight descends to bring some hope, one has to decide to stay in the gloom of fear or to accept the hope and run with it. Such a moment of decision is not all that rare. Most people find their days populated with both fear and hope, regarding even the smallest issues of life. For some, it is too confusing to know what to do. But for Claire, freedom from fear represented a choice she wanted to make and would do so over and over each day of her life. She had a long habit of depression, but she had decided to be happy. Would she have the strength to resist fear everyday? Would she declare herself willing and capable of being happy and walk over that bridge of despair to find what good happens next?

As it turned out, each day she lived in the duplex with her family of friends, she had more reasons to be happy, but still many reasons to be depressed. Some days, she was sure of a better future and other days, she doubted all of it. But since she had kept a diary for herself even as a child, she saw her notebook as an extension of an old enjoyable habit. She was careful to write her conversations accurately and completely.

When she got answers for questions she had asked, she recorded them. First she wrote her name and her question and then she wrote Soul Self and waited for an answer, which when it came, was always wise and beneficial.

She saved the notes from the first days after her discovery of the two minds.

Claire: Thanks for the great bread idea. It has helped me a lot.

Soul Self: You are welcome.

Claire: What else do you have for me?

Soul Self: Many good things.

Claire: Will it always be good?

Soul Self: Yes. All good, no harm.

Claire: What do I need to do to always hear you?

Soul Self: Be peaceful.

The more she worked with the dialogues, the easier and easier they became. She compared her earlier notes to those made a few weeks later.

Claire: I understand you are the higher mind of my soul. I have heard your thoughts before, but never realized how important they were. So why did it all become clear and so much easier now?

Soul Self: Because you asked to be happy.

Claire: Did I? I don't remember. Let me see, oh yes, it was the first note I made in my notebook: *I just want to be happy*. But I don't understand why that is so important.

Soul Self: Intention is everything. You intended to be happy, but how could you be happy not knowing your better half, so to speak, loving you and helping you to solve all of your problems? In short, you asked to be happy and a better contact with me was the fastest and easiest way to make you happy, so that's what happened. It works the same for anyone. Next question.

Claire: Makes sense, but Thelma has been able to hear spirit thoughts all of her life and she didn't know about the two minds. Why is my experience different than hers?

Soul Self: Her intention was different. She once lived in a house turned into a church and she thought about all of the people who'd died and been buried in the cemetery. She wanted to say hello to them, so that's what happened.

Claire: What about Alexa?

Soul Self: Her intention is to be a proficient user of Higher Mind for the benefit of historians, so that's what happened for her.

Claire: So does everything people intend happen just the way they intend?

Soul Self: Yes.

Claire: What if someone intended something bad, like blowing up an airplane?

Soul Self: Then it would happen unless other people intervene with a better intention. But no one who intends good for themselves would ever be hurt unless they thought being involved would be a good thing, which some do.

Claire: What could be good about being blown up in an airplane by terrorists?

Soul Self: The supposed victims unconsciously thought drawing international attention to the need for peace was a good thing. They arrived safe and sound with us in spirit form to help make peace over and over again. Nice folks to know, don't you think?

Claire: I never thought about it that way. Doesn't everyone intend good for their own lives?

Soul Self: Some do and some don't. Some do some of the time and not other times. Some just doubt themselves so much they don't make any decision about their intentions. It is indeed confusing.

Claire: OK, here is an important question for me. Most of my adult life, I have had some good and some bad things happen to me. Does that mean that I intended bad for myself?

Soul Self: Sometimes you intended good but then at other times, you lost confidence you were loved and therefore deserved good things to happen for you. In essence, you set no intention for good and accepted your apparently sad fate. The passing of your parents was a time for you to decide what you wanted for your life and now after many discouraging experiences, you have made a decision. You asked to be happy. It is an excellent decision and that is exactly what will happen without fail.

Claire: Who's going to make it happen?

Soul Self: We are together, of course. We will cooperate in full communication and love. It will be a piece of cake.

Claire: What? Was that you who sent the truck with the cake sign? How did you do that? Why did you do that?

Soul Self: Yes, I did that in order to encourage you. It was done through cooperation.

Claire: I wonder what else you can do.

Soul Self: You'll see soon enough.

Claire concluded that when good things begin to happen, it is apparently best not to question the process. Doubt creates confusion. Confusion causes a mix of good and bad events to happen. Most people would call it good and bad luck and have no idea why it all happens that way. But after rereading her notes, she decided life was not happenstance, luck or a statistical probability, but rather an orderly process of cause and effect. One's intentions are the cause and the effects are the events of one's life needed to fulfill that intention. Indeed it represented cooperation between the giver of the intention and the giver of the effects. In short, life is not automatic or mechanical, it is personal, very personal, between one's two minds.

Each day Claire looked forward to making her bread and taking care of Alexa and Alexa her. During the day, she spent her time helping around the house and on Thursdays making bread for Friday's farmer's market. With just a little more free time, she signed up for a community recreation department art class. She'd always wanted to try her hand at painting and with the supplies being inexpensive, she chose the free one-day sample class with the option to sign up for the whole course in the fall.

After a couple of weeks of selling the rosemary bread at the market, people were talking about it and her sales increased steadily. She was indeed earning more money, setting it aside to pay Thelma some rent. One day, a handsome black woman stopped by the booth.

"I hear you make a pretty good loaf of bread," said Gwen, smiling. "I'm the owner of Gwen's Bakery. Can I have a sample?"

"Sure, have a slice with some butter," offered Claire. "By the way, do you have a delivery truck with a cake sign on the side saying 'It's a piece of cake?'"

"Yes, have you seen it?" asked Gwen, eating the sample. She was a woman with lots of small business savvy and knew how to advertise her products and please customers.

"It came by our house at just the right time one day and I noticed it," said Claire, choosing not to explain why the sign was so meaningful to her.

"Your bread is wonderful. I can see you've really perfected it. This is a very special loaf of bread, made with love. It would be welcome in my shop. Is there any chance you might be interested in a job?" inquired Gwen. " I've had someone leave for another position and I need somebody part-time who really loves to make bread."

Claire momentarily held her breath, remembering how her Soul Self had said that she'd soon find out what kind of good can be done by them cooperating together. She struggled to look calm and said, "Why yes, I would love to work part-time. I take care of my friend's granddaughter after school, but I can work mornings most days."

"Good, we can work out the hours. Come to the bakery Monday morning and fill out our application. We'll see if we can pull it together," said Gwen, handing her business card to Claire.

"I have a feeling it'll work out very well. It'll be easy, like a piece of cake," Claire said, smiling, as did Gwen. They knew they shared a common love of baking and instinctively wanted to work together.

"See you then," called Gwen cheerfully as she left. Claire felt like pinching herself to be sure this conversation had really happened. It had only been a short time since she had been laid off from the dentist's office and now she was being offered a job doing something she loved, working for someone she liked. She crossed her fingers and made an X over her heart, something she and her mother had done when they wanted to say, *Thanks, I love you*. Then she shouted aloud, "Whoopee!" She was at that moment happy, just as she had intended.

+

Gwen's Bakery was located at the corner of Main and Evergreen in a hundred-year-old building that had been remodeled over and over again. Over the years, it had been a post office, a pharmacy, a restaurant and now a very good bakery. On Monday morning, Gwen welcomed Claire and outlined the job. Claire filled out the application and Gwen discussed her hours and pay, showing the corkboard where the scheduled hours for the week were posted each Monday. She agreed to work 7:30 to 2 four days a week, for starting pay. While she was in the shop, Claire sampled their bread, coffee and Danish and examined the equipment and display cases. After an hour, she left with the job and a good feeling about the decision. She would start yet this week.

Wearing her new apron, Claire started work at the bakery on Wednesday. She found the equipment to be basic, well used, but clean and functional. Her first task of the day was to mix the bread dough recipes in the big dough machine and then put the dough into pans to rise and later be baked. When the shop opened and people came in for morning pastries, she helped to tend the counter. She found the cash register a bit confusing to operate, but the other workers had developed a cheat sheet of instructions to keep her out of too much trouble. After the morning rush of customers, she cleaned the kitchen and baked the bread when it was ready. While still warm, she put the loaves in wax paper wrappers for the display case. The pay was minimal, but the work was enjoyable and the company of the other workers great.

Besides the owner, Gwen, the other employees included Ed and Mrs. Greene. Ed did just about everything and anything except bake, including driving the delivery truck. Mrs. Greene did cakes, pastries and cupcakes. Gwen did everything else, running the business in the simplest way possible. Beyond that, everyone did anything needed to make the bakery a success, taking care to do the best job possible. They knew everybody who came to the shop, whom they greeted with friendliness, laughing and teasing each other about everything.

After Claire became proficient at using the dough machine for the bakery's standard bread, Gwen asked her to adapt her rosemary recipe until she was satisfied it was truly great. Claire got many good suggestions for this effort from her Soul Self and when all agreed it was ready, Gwen ran a special offer on Claire's braided rosemary bread. Customers sampled it and started buying it regularly. Soon, it was an expected item for the display case.

In fact, all of the suggestions from her Soul Self were excellent and Ed and Mrs. Greene began to notice the improvements. They saw when she was confronted with a problem she would just stop and wait and then know the answer. They started asking her other questions for which she would wait for a minute and then give the answer. Thinking the ideas were pretty good, they tried them, never asking how she got the answers. They assumed, because she had some college, she was just smarter than most people, and so they respected her, as did Gwen. The net effect was that since business had been improving, there might be a bonus for everyone. In addition, with this kind of success, Gwen asked Claire and Ed to set up a booth for the bakery at the farmer's market and sell the bread and sweet baked goods to attract new customers to the bakery. They all worked to make this possible and life, as usual, went on pleasantly at the bakery.

+

Working in a small business and living in an old ethnic neighborhood of Cincinnati used to mean things peacefully continued generation after generation with little change. These neighborhoods had originally been small ethnic towns founded by immigrants, but they later expanded finally touching borders. Such towns became the bigger city of Cincinnati. These neighborhoods had always been comfortable and safe places to live, especially for families. But in the last forty years, the little communities had seen their share of tragedies such as what had happened to Annabelle.

Like many other children of the community, Thelma's daughter had been raised with the best of intentions, good discipline and work ethic the parents could muster. However, Annabelle and her peers were the first generation to be raised on a steady stream of graphic portrayal of movie and TV violence, exaggerated sexuality, drugs and crime. Before such media portrayals, most children in the town would have had no idea such options existed. It wasn't that anyone intended such drama and entertainment to do harm, but the introduction of the dramatic portrayal of the intention to do crime, drugs and risky sexual behaviors had planted seeds of intentions, which some young people nurtured, even if most did not. In short, these children had more harmful intentions from which to choose than previous generations.

Annabelle had selected the vice of her choice and engaged in the use and sale of drugs in the company of a like-minded young man with whom she became pregnant. She was very successful at crime, finding it satisfied her need for attention, money and rebellion. Later she became the leader of the local drug gang.

Despite Annabelle's self-destructive choices, Thelma determined to protect her daughter and future granddaughter from harm. She prayed to God day and night that both be rescued from harm and brought to a good life. She didn't care exactly how it would happen, but she wanted both to be safe and able to have another chance at being happy.

And so it happened, as Annabelle was making the biggest drug buy of her career, she was caught by an undercover police officer, arrested and taken to jail where she was to remain until she gave birth. While there, she gave the term *unruly inmate* a new meaning, and her baby was given to Thelma's care while she faced her trial and sentencing. Her public defender expected she would get the standard five years in prison for such offenses, but after verbally abusing the judge in a highly personal and insulting way in the courtroom and fighting with the guards suggesting they also do highly personal and insulting things to themselves, Annabelle was given an additional five years. They carried her from the courtroom literally kicking and screaming in rage.

Thelma, being a realist, knew the outcome was the best good that could be done. The baby was safe and Annabelle off the streets. Grateful both were alive and safe, she proceeded to raise Alexa to have a normal, happy childhood with a good life ahead of her. That's how, ten years later, the upstairs apartment and a pre-adolescent Alexa converged with Claire's need for a home and family.

Claire and her co-workers heard similar stories everyday as customers came and went for their coffee, pastries and bread. Claire prayed for each person, asking that good be done for them, but still didn't truly understand why or how bad things happen to people and how prayer could help. With so much pain and suffering in the world, surely there could be some way to end it, she thought. At least for her part, she held tightly to her clear intention for herself and her family of Thelma, Alexa and even Annabelle, to be happy.

The first week she and Ed took the bakery products to the farmer's market, they set up the bakery sign on the tables and arranged the baked goods for display. Claire was proud to be there on behalf of Gwen's bakery. Shortly the German man came around to see her. He commented on the display and asked if she had made any pretzel bread this week. She said no, but that she would keep it in mind. She offered him a sample of the rosemary bread and he liked it. Then she talked about some of the thoughts she had learned from the little book about fear. He cut her off and replied: "Look, lady, did I ask for any advice from you? I am what I am. Just leave me alone." Claire guessed he was unaware he was repelling her kindness and didn't take offense, but he kept talking, like he always did, covering up his fears.

"Well, then, can I sell you a pie or a few Danish?" she said politely.

"Never touch the stuff," he said and walked off unaware he had chosen once again to rebuff friendliness and to be alone. *How sad*, thought Claire. *I hope he finds some happiness somehow.*

The rest of the market was a great success, with little to bring back to the bakery other than the proceeds. Gwen was pleased. Together the employees discussed various ways to draw more customers to the bakery on a daily basis. Soon they had a plan to offer a coupon during the farmer's market for people to come to the shop for a free coffee and Danish. There, customers would be treated to warm friendliness, good products and service. Good ideas such as this seemed to be paying off and indeed they continued in great abundance because they all intended it to be that way.

Returning home after the market, Claire fixed supper so Thelma could rest her legs, which were hurting her so badly she wanted to sit for the evening. With green beans from the market and some leftover ham and hash browns for their supper, the threesome discussed the Saturday night school dance.

"Alexa, tell Diana that Claire and I will drive you and Cassie to and from the dance," said Thelma. "It starts at eight and we'll stay and work the punch and cookie table. We'll be home by ten-thirty." Thelma was very strict with Alexa about social occasions, knowing drugs are everywhere, but especially at school functions. If she could frisk each person coming and going, she would, but instead of embarrassing the girls, she used the punch table as an observation post to watch everything in the old school gym. In her mind, Alexa would NOT go down the path Annabelle had.

"OK, that sounds good to me," replied Alexa. "I'll let her know." Thelma was grateful Alexa trusted her and did not object to her intense protectiveness. Alexa's mother, Annabelle, had so rebelled against Thelma, they argued all of the time and nothing went right between them. After one such argument, Annabelle had run away from home, saying she would do exactly what she wanted to do, no matter what Thelma said. The memories of the event were a sorrow still residing in Thelma's heart, and she was not going to let her relationship with Alexa take a similar path.

Thelma reminded Alexa that Sunday was once again visiting day at the prison and invited Claire to come as well. "Yes, I'd like to come," said Claire. Thinking about the trouble Annabelle had gotten herself into, she asked, " Do you think people deliberately choose bad things for themselves?"

"Well, Annabelle certainly did a great job of that," Thelma said flatly. "I tried and tried to change her ways, but she just tried even harder to do the worst for herself. I don't know where she gets her stubbornness from."

Alexa and Claire glanced at each other, smiling, but saying nothing. "I saw that," said Thelma and they all laughed. "Well, that only goes to prove that two stubborn people can be different. One can have good on her mind and the other bad. I guess, people can only choose for themselves."

"OK, but that raises another question in my mind," continued Claire. " Let's say someone is in trouble they chose for themselves. Can we pray for them and intend good? Which will happen for them, the good or the bad?"

All three thought for a minute and finally Thelma said, "Both. They get a bad that works out good."

"Yeah, I can *so* see that," said Claire. "But then, I've seen people who let other people do bad to them. Then they see the consequences and complain about it." This time Thelma and Alexa smiled together, comparing Claire's words to her own situation.

Claire just had to say, "I saw that."

"Just who do you think was praying for you? Hint, hint." said Thelma.

"OK, it was you two. Thanks," replied Claire. Then after a moment, " What if we pray for Annabelle, what do you think will happen?"

"I don't know if the good overpowers the bad or if people change their minds and just start to want good things to happen for them," wondered Thelma. "You'd have to write in your notebook on that question. For me, I'm going to soak in a warm tub of Epson salts. My legs are killing me. Then I'm going to bed. Would you two clean up for me?"

The two started to clear the table and Thelma limped off to her room, muttering she should stop smoking. "Now that makes me think about illness," Claire started on a new question. "Can we pray for someone to be cured of some sickness or pain and have it happen? What do you think, Alexa?" Together they cleaned the kitchen, talking all of the time. Later they sat in the living room, watching documentaries about the profound mysteries of science, until Alexa went to her room to do her homework.

It was late when they all fell asleep. Claire had always prayed at night just as she had been taught as a child and that night fell asleep praying Thelma be cured of her painful leg problem. She had never had much response to prayers before, but to a Soul Self, listening in, a prayer made from such friendship was a call to action. To have such a prayer made in full confidence and without doubt was a rare opportunity not to be missed by the great family of souls, so much good was soon to come. Because of such good, Claire had crossed the bridge of despair and walked away wanting to be happy in the good company of her friends. It was to be a great journey not to be missed, but contained many unexpected events.

Chapter 7:
What Are the Right Words?

Although Claire slept well, by about 3 a.m. she became aware that her dreams had turned into a long conversation between her Soul Self and her half-awake human self. The conversation was all about making choices. She was thinking questions and getting long and interesting answers, sort of like a stream of consciousness in a good novel. She didn't even open her eyes. She just lay there, relaxed, letting it flow for the next two hours. The communication was an intimate conversation between the two parts of herself on a topic she'd been wondering about. But, it came so softly and quickly she could not remember most of it when she finally got up at 5. Because she was committed to recording her conversations with Soul Self, she turned on the light, sat up in bed with her notebook and pen on her lap and wrote as much as she could remember.

Claire: I've had enough of being sad and seeing everybody else in pain. I see so much pain and suffering in the world, I don't want anything to do with it. How can I avoid being sad ever again? On top of that, I want all people to be happy.

Soul Self: And so it will be. By requesting others be happy, it is apparent you have a true intention to be happy. For how can you be happy when others suffer? To request it for other people is to request all higher minds be at work on the issue and all human minds be in cooperation. It will take billions of souls and their cooperating human partners, so it will take some time, but as soon as the right words are used, it will be much easier.

Claire: First, I thank you for the sure knowledge that it can be so. But you said something very interesting at the end and I just have to ask, *What are the right words to make all people happy?*

Soul Self: To get the best results, you must ask to be happy, truly happy. To be happy because you are no longer sad is not really being happy. You can no longer even have sad memories of bad things in the past. You don't remember it, but we intended for you to be truly happy in this lifetime. Could you try to name all of your life experiences as having some happiness leading to more?

Claire: You just took a left turn I didn't expect. When did we decide all of this?

Soul Self: Before you incarnated, we made a life plan and we are working together on it now.

Claire: Really? I am sad some of the time and angry and at other times, I am happy. The doctor thinks I have depression. Is that my life plan?

Soul Self: Your life plan is to end all sadness. Your end of the bargain is to refuse to be fearful. Call yourself a person who is in the process of being happy and you have already called yourself happy.

Claire: OK, I see your point and I do admit I have looked at myself in the mirror each day and given myself sad labels. Maybe I was increasing my sadness by saying I was sad. But you're saying more than that. You're suggesting I've never had a sad thing happen to me. This sounds crazy, as I can immediately think of so many sad and unloving events. I want to try what you suggest, so how do I do this?

Soul Self: Remember your inquiry about helping others with prayers and healing another's illness and pain? Ask us that question again and form the question with great confidence.

Claire: OK, that's a good idea. *Give me the words I need to assure the healing of pain and suffering so we can all be happy.*

Soul Self: Well stated! Your intention is clear and without doubt and does not require any specifics or timeframes. You can simply state the need of the people you have in mind and tell me to make them happy. Then you are done and I take over.

Let me illustrate with a little story. Before you were born, there was a man who wanted to be the inventor of something that would protect a wound and promote its healing. Thus his Soul Self sent him all of the materials and expertise needed to put together a product for rapid wound healing, the adhesive bandage, and it worked very well. However, in your case, you did not ask to be the healer giving treatments or to be the inventor of medical supplies or treatments. You did not even ask to know how the healing would be done. You asked that I take care of all of it and thus it will be so.

Great healers always have time on their hands and yet heal hundreds and even thousands of people with no effort at all. They use their intentions in the highest way possible in cooperation with their highest and wisest soul family. In short, they do it the easy way.

Now, let's apply this to your own depression. Do you want it healed?

Claire: Yes, most certainly.

Soul Self: Do you want us to do it painlessly and with little additional effort or worry or do you want the fear and grief to continue longer?

Claire: No, I don't need the whole thing drawn out. You do it the fast and easy way, your way.

Soul Self: OK, then it is done. Now do you see how having the sad times in your life has led you to discover one of the great healing miracles in the physical universe? Would you do it again to have such a gift, knowing sadness would have no real effect on you or your health?

Claire: Well, yes, I guess so. But is it necessary to be sick to learn how to cure sickness?

Soul Self: No, it's not necessary. In your case, you needed to be depressed to see that an alternative was available, but now it is no longer necessary. It all comes down to how stubbornly an individual believes in his or hers own unworthiness. Now that you've seen how being healthy and happy is so easy and being sick is not necessary, you can now stubbornly believe in your own good fortune. Can you now see the depression as a means to happiness? In fact, it has been a joy, hasn't it, to come to this moment.

Claire: Stubborn? How was I stubborn in believing my own unworthiness? OK, you don't have to answer that. I know I was down on myself and didn't make good decisions when I could have. But how did I finally get the courage to change?

Soul Self: Your friends helped you to release your fears. They offered you some love and support, first through their prayers for you and later with the offer of a place to live. They even made you a part of their family. That is what you intended when you called Thelma to tell her about the debts, wasn't it?

Claire: I hoped so, but I didn't know so. Did you have something to do with it?

Soul Self: Certainly. Thelma always asks for help from her Soul Self. When she got the message to invite you to live with her, she saw it would help all concerned. The rest is history.

Claire: I see. So are you saying a friend who can converse with Soul Self is the best friend of all?

Soul Self: Yes. Are you not wide-awake early in the morning writing in this notebook trying to find a way for Thelma to be healed of her leg problems? You are using the help of your Soul Self for her benefit, just as she did hers for you. Sounds like love being given back and forth, doesn't it?

Claire: Yes, it does. I guess you could say, we are friends getting help from friends in high places. That's sort of funny, but really, it's profound. So how do I help her leg problem?

Soul Self: The same way you helped your own illness. Just ask that she be happy, which of course would require she be healthy and active. Then think no more about it except to feel good about your intention. Let us do the rest.

Claire: Will it work? How does it work?

Soul Self: Her life path is a good one, but there are a few fears that keep her uncomfortable. We will be removing them and thus the discomfort. The second question is for another day and another notebook.

Claire: What is her fear?

Soul Self: That she is not quite up to bringing a successful result from all of this trouble.

Claire: OK. By the way, should Thelma and I continue to go to the doctor or can you cure people without any medical care?

Soul Self: Yes, go to the doctor. She will prescribe the standard treatment and follow up with counseling sessions to confirm your health. That will make you all the happier. Never deny yourself good care. We also talk to doctors who listen to us. Now, set your intention for all the care that you need to be available, helpful and never give harm or stress.

Claire: Done. I set the intention for all of the care I need be available, helping me with no harm. Wait a minute! Isn't that the Hippocratic oath doctors take? They swear to do no harm and to heal the patient? That's interesting.

Soul Self: Yes, that oath comes from the Greek tradition, which was founded on the teachings of the ancient Egyptians who learned it from us. Fancy meeting you here, after so long a time. Do you realize you were part of that ancient teaching?

Claire: Really? I hope it still works today. So tell me about praying for Annabelle, who has stubbornly held to bad intentions. What can we do for her?

Soul Self: We can do the same thing. You set the intention for her happiness and we will do the rest. With her level of resistance and fear, it will be slow progress with some events designed to turn her in a new direction, but she will now be on a clear path to resolution.

She's chosen the hard way to be happy and you the easy way. Stubbornness in choosing unhappiness is like resisting the progress of the stars, it only wears out the stubborn one. In essence, we provide everyone with happiness all of the time. If it is refused or blocked by fear, we apply more and deeper happiness until the dam overflows and opens up the closed heart. This is how the universe is wired.

Claire: What about people who pray for healing and don't get healed?

Soul Self: Some come to their illnesses for another purpose which is in their life plan, but if they ask to be happy, they will be.

Claire: Very cool! I get that. I hereby intend Annabelle be happy so we all get to enjoy it as well. I can't believe how confident I feel. I'm starting to get a picture of how powerful you are.

Soul Self: Actually, you haven't seen anything. Have a great day. Talk to you later.

Saturday, the day of the school dance, was beautiful and sunny. After a flurry of normal weekend cleaning and shopping duties, Claire took Cassie and Alexa to the shopping center beauty shop to get haircuts and styling. Both Claire and Thelma had learned long ago this beauty shop was essentially a gossip shop with the client's hair receiving only leftover attention at best, as was the prevailing intention of the staff. However, with Claire's specific instructions as to style and price, it was a pleasant afternoon and the girls came out looking great. When they returned home, Thelma was pleased and the girls trotted off to Cassie's house to show Diana the net effect and play their favorite games.

Later that evening, Claire, Thelma and the two girls arrived at the school dance, comfortable in their fashion choices. A DJ was playing music, while young boys and girls roamed around the gym floor talking to each other. Some were actually dancing, but not with each other.

"See the girl with the pink dress? That's Brandon's sister, Shelly. She's really good in math," Alexa informed Claire and Thelma working at the punch bowl table. "There's Wendy by the vending machines. I like her. Over by the door are her mother and father."

Cassie joined in. "I like Brandon. I think he's cute. Shelly told me he likes dogs."

"Are any of your teachers here?" asked Claire.

"There's Mrs. Hudson. She's my history teacher. And beside her is the principal, Mr. Willowby."

"Do you want to dance?" Cassie asked Alexa. They both began to dance on the gym floor in a group of boys and girls. The DJ invited others to join the group and soon there was a teeming ball of movement twisting and turning, giving the party its best moments. Later, many dancers retired to the punch table where Thelma talked to them, learning their names and families. It was a successful night of the kind ten and eleven-year-olds enjoy.

As the party-goers returned home from the dance, Cassie's parents accompanied by their dog Shadow, joined them for ice cream at Thelma's house. After a thorough recap of the dance, Cassie and her family left. Later, the two girls talked on the phone about their friends for yet another hour until Thelma called for lights out. Even after that, they texted secretly under the covers for yet another hour.

As the evening was warm, Thelma sat on the front porch, for once not smoking, and contemplated her own early dating and marriage. Would she ever entertain another male companion? What would that be like? Claire, in her own room, was thinking the same thing. Neither woman was brave enough to ask for such a thing because they knew if they asked for it, it might happen. For now, their doubts and fears of relationships were just too strong to overcome.

Without Claire even asking a question, her Soul Self sent the thought, *Asking for something that seems scary and dangerous to you would never work out well. You need to find better words.* She picked up her notebook and pen and started writing.

Claire: I know you're talking to me. I am doing better and am less depressed, so would another relationship be in my best interest? Would it make me happy?

Soul Self: No, not at this time. If a relationship would make you happy, it would have been given at the right time. No sense in worrying about it now, is there? Do you trust me to handle this for you?

Claire: Now there's a good question. Trust? How do I ever come to trust my future again? I'm beginning to see how you're always on my side, always helpful, very wise and indeed far more powerful to make things happen than I can understand, but what about the sad things that happen in life, everyone's life? Would you ever send pain and suffering to test me or teach me, or something like that?

Soul Self: No, never. If you are being stubbornly miserable, we might send attention-getting events to turn you in a better direction, if that's what you mean. Also, sometimes people do difficult and painful things out of love for others. But even in those circumstances, we make sure no real harm happens. Soul Selves are incapable of giving harm, mainly because it does not exist for us to give.

Claire: So it gets back to cooperating and not resisting happiness. Let's just say I managed to be highly cooperative about being happy in all matters, then what would happen?

Soul Self: Without any resistance, we could deliver good times in constant expansion until you were so joyful you would be more like us and give it all away to others. Want to give it a try?

Claire: Here we go again. I know I will be losing my mind again, but I have to say yes. Why would I deliberately say no? I will give no resistance to being happy, since you always send me good things that will grow and expand into joy. How's that?

Soul Self: Entirely sufficient. We are becoming great friends, aren't we? Neither of us wants anything but the highest good for each other. With your intention and cooperation and my power, good things will inevitably happen. That was easy, wasn't it? Now maybe you should rest. We have a lot to do to heal your body and those of your loved ones for whom you requested health and happiness, and we like to do our healing during sleep when there is little resistance. Night, night.

Claire: Goodnight.

Claire realized this conversation might be considered weird by the standards of some people who would think it very naive to believe a wonderful benign spirit entity would heal her of depression. It was even more preposterous to believe the same could be done for others. Finally, to think that, for the rest of her life, she would never experience harm just because she asked for it to be so, was a great leap of faith in a spirit being whose thoughts she could only know in her mind.

For the time being, however, she didn't much care how strange it might seem. If it proved to be true, then she had discovered something precious and meaningful to her. The world could be a happy place for friends to be good friends. She crawled into bed and slept a long and forgetful sleep, during which she did indeed lose her mind, only to awake with a happier one.

Chapter 8:
Intention is Everything

While Claire slept, she dreamed of Abraham Lincoln making a speech on the battlefield with only one person present, a wounded soldier. Lincoln said, *When in the course of human events it becomes necessary for a nation to decide what kind of better life they might want to lead, then the rules suddenly change and something different starts to happen. The pursuit of happiness has its own way of unfolding and demanding change of a benign kind, flowing from the heart in joy. The wisdom to know what to do or how to do it comes from another, higher source, but we as a people are now free from the slavery of fear. We choose to be happy.* The president stopped speaking, put on his tall hat and stepped down from the podium, waving to the soldier to go home. When she awoke, she felt like that soldier being sent home to return to his family. It felt like the war was over.

Sunday was monthly family visiting day at the state prison. Having gone there for many years, Thelma and Alexa knew what to expect and usually dreaded it. Today Claire was going to accompany them and she had no idea what it would be like.

As the three drove the sixty miles to the state prison, they talked about Annabelle and her life. Thelma, as a single mother, had raised Annabelle with only occasional influence from the girl's father, Steve. He had moved out of town and was rarely in touch with Thelma, and even when he visited, Annabelle would always be upset. If only Thelma knew what had gone on between them.

Annabelle had been a healthy and robust baby, but always one for temper tantrums. She had a strong personality even as a two-year-old, which developed into longstanding rebellion. The frequent battles of will between Thelma and Annabelle were vivid events and became a way of life for the child, who battled each and every teacher, principal and police officer she ever met. The only peers who agreed with her conflict with authority were those who regularly sought out trouble. And so, even in grade school, trouble was her best friend.

But there were some happy times as well. One Christmas Thelma bought the four-year-old Annabelle a beautiful red dress to wear to a Christmas party with her preschool friends. Annabelle felt very happy and pretty with her dark red hair and snappy eyes attracting attention in the dress.

There were times when the two went for walks in the park and Thelma pointed out flowers and birds, trying to teach Annabelle their names, but to no avail. Thelma always made good and nutritious meals and unsuccessfully tried to teach the child the basics of cooking. But always on Annabelle's birthdays, Thelma made a special meal with homemade birthday cake and gifts. It all could have been so good.

At fifteen, Annabelle won the part of the Witch of the West in *The Wizard of Oz* in her school drama production. She was a natural, Thelma said with, a wry smile and some sorrow. The after-play party proved to be a turning point in Annabelle's life, as someone brought drugs and offered them to the cast and crew. Most of the children declined them, but Annabelle wanted to try them to see how it felt. And it felt oh, so good. This first experiment was to lead to more.

By the time of her High School graduation, Annabelle knew her way around the local drug culture and had sampled all types of drugs. Her clever mind, good looks and bold confrontation with people won her the leadership of a drug gang. She was enthralling to be with and quickly learned to control people for her own purposes. Then came Tim, the love of her life, or so it seemed at age twenty. He was handsome, rode a motorcycle and carried a gun in his saddlebags. Together they were a modern rendition of Bonnie and Clyde with much to enjoy and to do that was wicked at an early age. They both anticipated a long future of thrills ahead for them.

When she found herself to be pregnant, she and Tim initially thought a baby would be a wonderful thing, but as the pregnancy proceeded, they tired of the inconvenience of the whole thing. Thelma demanded Annabelle go to a treatment center for the health of the baby, but she would have none of it. However the disagreement was soon resolved when Annabelle showed up for a large drug buy. Unfortunately or fortunately, depending on how one looked at it, the seller was an undercover police officer, who immediately arrested her.

Annabelle was sent to a women's prison hospital where she was treated for addiction and received excellent prenatal care. There she delivered her baby girl and named her Annabelle after herself. Thelma was present at the birth and seeing the beautiful and perfect little girl, vowed to herself this granddaughter would never follow in Annabelle's path. And so following the birth, Thelma petitioned the court to be allowed to adopt the baby and change her name to Alexa, after her great grand mother, Alexandra. The judge requested an investigation by social services, which documented Annabelle's long record of rebellion and drug use and the prospect of a long prison sentence. The social worker declared her an unfit mother and that's how Thelma was awarded custody of Alexa.

In time, Annabelle recovered and appeared at her hearing and later her sentencing. Annabelle heard the long list of offenses of which she was accused and was amazed how much the justice system knew about her activities. At the sentencing, she was given five years, to which she laughed and told the officers to get their hands off of her. She declared herself free to do whatever she wanted and produced a deluge of abusive profanity directed towards the judge, who realized five years would probably have little effect on her. That's how she got ten years.

At the state prison, Annabelle fell into line with other prisoners worse than herself and failed every parole hearing. She never could convince the parole board she meant to be clean of drugs and lead a good life. This being the last year of her sentence, she would be up for release soon. Thelma secretly feared Annabelle, if released, would die an early death or simply disappear, but she prayed for a much better outcome.

Thelma and Alexa were in the front seats of Thelma's tiny red economy car. From the back seat, Claire asked some questions which caused the two in the front seat to say aloud what they had both been thinking for the last few years.

"So why do you think Annabelle turned to a life of crime and danger you tried so hard to avoid?" asked Claire.

Thelma had asked herself this question many times and had a ready answer, which usually gave her some peace. "It's our life paths to be together and to have these experiences."

Alexa's answer was a little different. "She thinks she's like her father."

After thinking this over, Claire offered, "What if she thinks that she's like her father and then later changes her mind?"

Thelma spoke, but both she and Alexa agreed with the same thought: "She can, but she does not have the right to make our lives miserable in the meantime. If she makes harm, then she has to bear the consequences. We've made a good life for ourselves and we won't let her interfere."

"What would you say if she changed her mind to be good?"

Alexa supplied Thelma's most likely response, "It's about time!" They all laughed and silently prayed for such a day.

Silence then resumed and a kind of peace. None of the three looked forward to seeing Annabelle in prison and listening to her angry rendition of prison life, the staff and inmates, but they were her family and they cared about her. In their minds, they wanted her to be a beautiful woman with a good future.

The visit, as usual, went something like this:

Thelma and Alexa said hello and asked how Annabelle was.

Annabelle replied she was terrible for many reasons and proceeded to blame everyone else for what annoyed her.

Thelma changed the subject, trying to make neutral conversation. They discussed the other inmates, the prison school and of course the half-way house.

Thelma ended the visit early saying they prayed for her and hoped she would do well.

Annabelle shrugged her shoulders and laughed.

Claire said very little during the visit, but she did learn Annabelle had been taking a course in cosmetology so as to have a trade after prison. Annabelle liked working with hair and had fixed her own beautiful dark auburn hair in a very becoming style. Claire also learned Annabelle had found a few grey hairs on her temples, and wondered if Annabelle thought about getting old, sitting in prison. The ride home was, gratefully, a much happier time than the visit.

"Did you notice how pretty Mom's hair was?" Alexa said.

"Yeah, it was great. She has a talent with hair," said Claire. "Wonder what she thought of our hair?"

"Well, first thing," said Alexa, intending to tease both of them, "you both wear old-fashioned styles. Why don't you try something new?"

"There was a day when I tried all kinds of things," said Thelma, "but nothing ever seemed to work. "

"Same here," said Claire. "My hair has a mind of it's own. I keep my hair comfortable in a ponytail. That's the best I can do."

"You'll probably do the same thing when you get to be our age," teased Thelma.

"I don't think so," said Alexa in her best Valley Girl gestures and intonations. As they all laughed, Thelma turned up the music on the car radio nice and loud and they all sang along with a hip-hop song. Laughter being required therapy for most problems in this family, it was likely to run a long time. Thus the ride home greatly improved the day.

Turning into the driveway, Thelma declared it so good to be home that she was going to fix spaghetti for supper, just as soon as she had her cigarette and cola. She could not, however, find her cigarettes, so she just had the cola and a rest on the porch swing.

Claire took the opportunity to go to her apartment and change clothes. She made a few notes in her notebook to remind her of some questions she wanted to ask, then quickly went down to Thelma's kitchen to start supper. Alexa, setting the table, warned her that Thelma was likely to start singing her best version of Italian opera. To preclude this, Alexa put a Frank Sinatra CD in the boom box and turned it up loud. They both laughed as they lip synched with Frank and soon it looked like there might be dinner and dancing this evening. Thelma returned from the porch, telling Claire to move over because she was going to make the garlic bread as only she knew how. Claire faked annoyance.

Soon the red sauce, the big bowl of spaghetti noodles and garlic bread were on the table. Before the assembled threesome began to fill their plates, they paused to say a prayer. Claire took the lead.

"God bless this meal and all who are part of this family, including Annabelle. May we all be happy. Amen."

"Amen. Amen. Amen." The dinner proceeded with gusto, all knowing that dancing and dirty dishes would follow, or maybe dirty dancing and clean dishes. Imagining the kitchen to be an Italian restaurant with Frank, himself, singing in front of a full orchestra, they honored his great love themes, proclaiming them as inevitably true. They made grand sweeps of imaginary long dresses around the table, holding spoons for microphones. Not surprisingly, Thelma, being in her element, was magic as she portrayed herself as the seductress of Siena, standing in a fountain.

The only thing that could have brought this party to an end was exhaustion and soon they rested on the porch, laughing at the lusts of life that romantic songs portray. Only as they cooled off in the encroaching cool evening air, did they realize how tired they really were. Later in the quiet of her own room, Claire wrote out her questions about the day and made some notes.

Claire: We had such a good time this evening! The day started as something we all dreaded, but it had such a happy ending. I saw true joy today!

Soul Self: Amazing how joy can spring from nothing but the impulse to make it, isn't it? And be encouraged, there are signs that Annabelle is moving towards a happier life. Her work with hairstyles constitutes no harm and much good. It is a small seed of happiness, but it will grow. Also she sees she is getting older and has begun thinking her life of youthful rebellion might not be so easy for her to continue. It is but a small recognition of the need for change, but it will grow.

Claire: How does Thelma really feel about her daughter?

Soul Self: She grieves the painful life Annabelle is facing, but she doesn't blame herself and won't let it do harm to her or Alexa. Thelma is a strong person with strong intentions. By the way, you helped Thelma a lot by saying the prayer before supper. Her Soul Self says thank you.

Claire: Are you talking to Thelma's Soul Self? I didn't realize that you all talk together about such small things. Tell me more.

Soul Self: We all know each other and, since we all love each other, we cooperate to help whenever we can. We are the Great Oneness, after all, and we have great fun together, just like your dinner and dancing.

Claire: The Great Oneness? I had no idea. Please tell Annabelle's Soul Self I will help if I can. Just let me know what I can do. By the way, how did Annabelle get such bad self-esteem when Thelma tried so hard to raise her right?

Soul Self: Her Soul Self says her father told her as a small child, she was just like him and she would never amount to anything good. In fact, you can talk to her Soul Self directly anytime and indeed she will send you word if there is anything more you can do to help.

Claire: Really? I can talk to another Soul Self? How do I do that and how many are there?

Soul Self: The first question is how. Remember intention is everything. Just address a Soul Self in a friendly way, asking for something good and wait for a reply. The second question is how many we number. There are many more than you could ever count and they are all related to each other, congregating in groups and families. Usually, one's own Soul Self acts as the one to make introductions to the others. Once again we do it by cooperation. It's a piece of cake.

Claire: Oh!

Soul Self: I see that you are fatigued and need some refreshment. Would you like to take a walk or just go to bed early?

Claire: Both.

Soul Self: OK. Then, I'll send you a little energy for a walk and later send you a gentle urge to sleep. You have made much progress today in understanding and, given your heartfelt desire to help another, we have given much good. I will make many adjustments in your body and emotions to rebalance your systems while you sleep. Have a nice evening. See you in your dreams.

Claire: See you in my dreams.

After Claire took a relaxing walk, she felt very much better. When she came home and was preparing for bed, she wondered how her Soul Self makes adjustments to her body and sees her in her dreams, but tonight she only had the energy to say thank you and ask for a good night's sleep. The stars winked in agreement and a cloud floated across the half moon like a crooked smile. All seemed at rest and so was she. She had learned a lot about intention and liked the part that once an intention has been set, one can then rest and let it work on its own. What was to follow would put that knowledge to a strong and memorable test.

Chapter 9:
Mirror, Mirror

After a very restful and deep night's sleep, Claire arose to begin her week. She had an appointment with her doctor to go over a treatment plan for her depression and then she would attend her first art class. The rest of the week would be consumed by the work at the bakery and chauffeuring Cassie and Alexa to the season's final soccer practices. Perhaps the week would be, as predicted, filled with good things getting better.

As was her habit of late, she looked in her bathroom mirror evaluating what she saw in her face. Would she see shadows of fear and sorrow or traces of hope for a No More Tears life? This morning she saw both and remembered what she had written in her notebook about making a decision as to where her life was directed. She wanted to declare that her depression and financial problems would vanish and never return to darken her future, but for now they were still present. How was she to be content in the meantime, teetering between her intention to be healed, supported by the power of the Soul Self to make it so, but the knowledge that in reality it was not yet so? How could she decide to be happy and healthy and deal with the fear she might possibly not succeed? Wouldn't failure crush her hope?

The mirror reflected all of her thoughts accurately. If she thought about disaster, her face turned pale and sad. If she thought about a good outcome, her face turned rosy and bright. So which person was she, the sad one or the bright one? At that confusing juncture of thought, she paused and waited for the now familiar feel of her Soul Self. After a moment, she recognized the suggestion, "Choose which you want to be, the facts will eventually come into compliance. Keep choosing what you want and you will do better than to doubt. The worst thing is to make no decision."

The suggestion got to the heart of her depression in a hurry and cleared out a new artery of hope. She did not want the sad face; she wanted the bright face. Therefore, she declared to her fearful mind that she wanted to be free and happy, even if the facts did not at first support her choice. She even allowed something different but very much better than she could imagine might transpire. She decided she would be open-minded and even unreasonably optimistic about it and refuse to dwell on doubt.

With that decision made, she brushed her teeth, fixed her hair, remembering but postponing Alexa's suggestion to try a new hairstyle, and then she dressed. She was now pretty good at getting up early enough to have breakfast with Alexa and see her off to school. Being helpful to Thelma gave her a strong sense of being needed and she enjoyed the child's wise company. Both lent urgency to her being healthy. The final thought about her future came out something like this: *I have too much good to live for to be sick and poor. In my mind, I want to be fine and that's final.*

After Alexa left, Claire drove to her doctor's appointment. Although she had decided she wanted a positive outcome, it felt much like holding back a dam of doubt. Having the appointment early today meant she had less time to deal with her doubt and anxiety threatening to loosen her plug in the dam of anxiety.

In the doctor's waiting room, she looked around at the people who were chatting about their latest surgery or diagnosis. Clearly some of them had much worse disabilities and problems than she. It gave her some comfort, but not for them, she thought. At least she had requested a healthy life and not just accepted the slow progression towards decline many did. Then she strongly felt that, if she could be successful, they could as well, prompting her to silently say a prayer for all of them to be well and happy.

Waiting alone in the exam room before the doctor comes in had always been uncomfortable to her, as her imagination typically would conjure all kinds of bad news and consequences, followed by sad questions and outcomes. It was hard for her to control such thoughts, but she did manage to say to herself repeatedly: *I am going to be fine. I am going to be fine.*

At last, Dr. Laura Connor, a very professional looking middle-aged woman arrived. She had an honest smile and a pleasant manner of talking to her patients that elicited reassurance. Her busy practice attested to her skill and experience.

"Hello, Claire. I'm glad to see you again. Let me review your file for a moment and we'll discuss your treatment. I see you were evaluated for depression at the time of your husband's death. How are you doing now?"

Claire caught her breath as she remembered his illness and death. "He was depressed and then he got cancer and died. I had to sell my house to pay the debts. I'm now living with some friends. Sometimes I feel so lost I don't know who I am, but other times, I feel pretty good."

94

Noting Claire's fears and grief, Dr. Connor said "Don't think his situation is the same as yours. Because you have depression does not mean you will necessarily have the other problems he had. But you are in a stressful life situation, which can make depression worse. Have you or any member of your family ever taken medication for depression?"

Claire managed to say, "No, and I don't want to take medications. I saw what they did to my husband and I don't want to be like that."

"I can see you have some misgivings about medications. Would you be interested in having some counseling sessions regarding your current situation and then we can reevaluate your depression later? I can write an order and it will be covered by insurance," Laura said compassionately. "Remember, Claire, right now everything looks fearful to you, but with some help and support, you will see things in a better light. Let's see how you are in a few weeks. After that, if you'd like, I'll give you a complete physical and order some tests so you can be reassured of your health situation. "

"I'd like that," said Claire, relaxing a bit.

" Very well, then, I'd like you to meet our counselor, Dr. Scott Brun. He will set you up with some appointments and I need to see that you keep them," instructed Dr. Conner taking charge of the situation.

"OK."

Dr. Connor made some notes on the computer and shook Claire's hand saying she would help her with all of her medical problems during this difficult time.

Claire began to be emotional after the doctor left the room. Sure that her worst fears were being addressed by someone who knew what she needed, she choked on the emotion of relief. Then the nurse came in and took her to another office in the building that was labeled Counseling Services where Dr. Brun worked.

In his office, she sat in a comfortable chair as Dr. Brun introduced himself, asking her to call him Scott. He outlined a series of sessions in which they would work together toward a goal and then report back to Dr. Connor. Claire liked the young man, but wondered how he could help her. He asked if she had any questions.

"So what would these sessions be like?" Claire inquired.

"First I'll ask some questions and get to know your history and then we'll identify a goal for us to work toward."

"I know what my goal is," blurted Claire. "I want to be happy!"

"Excellent!" smiled Scott, "That's my goal for you as well. We are off to a good start."

Claire smiled, thinking about her notes with Soul Self and began to feel her confidence. "So when is my first appointment?"

"What day is best for you? I have some morning appointments available."

"I work mornings at the bakery."

"How about next Monday afternoon?"

"Deal!" Claire felt surprisingly uplifted. Just as Soul Self had said, the medical care had done no harm and a lot of good. She got up to leave and Scott said he'd see her next week and did she need a reminder? She replied no, she always remembered something good.

Walking into the sunshine of the parking lot, Claire relaxed for a moment and looked up at the sky. She was glad she had come, but she now felt tired and yearned for the comfort of home, so she put her car in gear and headed back to Thelma's house. She just wanted to rock like a baby on her mother's lap and forget the grief of the last few years.

What she actually did was to lie down on the swing on the front porch and immediately fall asleep. The swing had comfortable cushions and a warm quilt and its lazy motion was very relaxing. She slept in the partial sun and mild breezes for more than an hour. She had no dreams, nor any recollection of time passing. She did not even remember who she was. She just slept.

Eventually, she came back to awareness and sat up to stretch her back and shoulders. Realizing she was thirsty and hungry, she went to the kitchen for a sandwich and a glass of water. There she found some chocolate chip cookies left by Thelma. These had been her mother's favorites to make for her and she wondered how Thelma knew to leave them for her today. Somehow that sandwich and those cookies were the most delicious ones she could ever remember eating. Everything seemed vivid, clear and perfectly beautiful. It was a strange, but wonderful awareness, as if she wasn't even herself, just a set of eyes looking at someone else's body. She felt safe and joyful, so she just enjoyed the feeling. Soon, feeling more energetic, she took a short walk around the yard, looking at the flowers, trees and grass in a whole new way.

"How could things be so beautiful?" she said to no one but herself. " I'm alive and will be OK, the sun is shining and flowers are blooming." She knew she was experiencing something special which led her to think about her notebook. She suddenly wanted to discuss the events of the day with her Soul Self, her dearest and best friend who had told her she would be fine and nothing bad was going to happen to her. She took a deep breath for the first time in a long time and laughed aloud. In fact, as she took the steps up to her apartment two at a time, shouting, "Whoopee!"

In her notebook, she recorded her conversation.

Claire: I can't believe this, but I'm going to get great help and will be fine. You were right. I was so afraid. I should have trusted you more.

Soul Self: No harm done and now you can see you have new options for much more that's good. That was our intention for this lifetime together and, in fact, for all time. People who discover their life plan is a good one call this intention The Highest Good.

Claire: So you are saying we both intended for me to have a good life with no harm? So why have I had such unhappiness?

Soul Self: How did you feel when you were in fear for your future? How did you see the world around you and yourself?

Claire: When I was fearful, I saw harm ahead for me and thought the world was a dangerous place. I thought others were trying to hurt me on purpose. OK, now I see your point. Looking into the mirror with fear, I see harm. Looking in the mirror with The Highest Good, I see good ahead. In fact, after I got good help from the doctor, I felt the world was beautiful. All of the flowers were intensely beautiful and the food intensely delicious. The mirror must work both ways. What was that all about?

Soul Self: You have said it well yourself. Fear yields harm and trust in good yields good, meaning very good. You can create your own harm with your fears making more fear. Or you can intend good and the good will create more good. You can have it either way, but you do have to choose one or the other. Do you see what we meant when we said intention is everything?

By the way, did you see me all around you in the mirror this morning? Did you see your aura?

Claire: My aura? What's that? What do you mean? I thought you were a spirit, which is invisible. Please explain.

Soul Self: Around your body is a powerful and beautiful energy field where I reside. Actually, we both live within it. At times it's visible as a wavy bit of disturbance in light, but in spirit form it's a ball of brightly colored energy. It's the same for every being. I tell you this to give you an idea of what life is really like. Your body is the condensed form of the energy in your aura wanting to be alive in the physical realm. What do you think of that?

Claire: I had no idea. I thought I only existed within my skin, but it sounds like the energy part of me is much bigger and you say more beautiful and powerful. So you live there with me in my aura? So does this mean we are roommates, like me and Thelma and Alexa? Interesting. I had no idea. What do you look like?

Soul Self: I look like an oval eggshell surrounding your body. Actually, you live within me and we both live within God's great uterus. We all consist of mind and energy and, in your case, mass.

Claire: Then mind is the common denominator among us. Then, I'll have to ask you to better define mind.

Soul Self: Better to say "self." A mind is the operating part of a self-thinking entity, reacting, deciding, communicating, questioning and indeed growing in awareness, all of the above and more. Being energy, a mind doesn't need a body to function, but in humans, it does have a nervous system and body to use in the physical realm.

When the body ceases to live, the mind just lifts out of the body and continues on as an energy form, doing the same as it did before it came to enliven the body at birth. Really very simple to understand once you realize that a mind, the Self, is indestructible because it is energy. Did you not feel for a moment today you were outside of your body looking at it?

Claire: Yes, I did. I wondered what that was all about. Are you saying that my mind stepped out for just a moment from my body?

Soul Self: Well, not very far and not for very long. Your mind shifted into our aura for a moment and then back. This experience should tell you your mind isn't limited to your nervous system. Really, it's simple to understand.

Claire: Yes, it seems simple, if you believe in a soul. I wish I could see the aura in which we live. Thelma says she sometimes can. Thank you for loving me and showing me how I can be healed. You are my best friend, my twin, my family and much more. I think this notebook is going to be a treasure for me.

+

When Thelma and Alexa joined Claire over the supper table, they congratulated her on her good news. Claire thanked Thelma for the cookies and described how reality seemed so clear and delicious to her for a few minutes. Thelma smiled, remembering a time when she had a similar experience.

Apparently, it was a common human event when emotions of joy run high.

Thelma paused for a long time and Claire and Alexa sensed something not so happy was going to be addressed next. After wondering what it was, both concluded silently it must be about Annabelle.

"I got a letter today saying Annabelle is going to be released in thirty days and we have to decide to arrange for her to stay in a halfway house for prison women or let her stay here," Thelma stated thoughtfully. " Do you still think she cannot stay here?"

"I don't want her coming here because she will bring the drug people to the house," said Alexa. Claire quickly seconded her opinion.

"I thought the same thing," said Thelma, "but is the halfway house the best thing?"

"Shouldn't we have compassion for her?" asked Claire, thinking about her religious training to help the unfortunate.

Thelma leaned towards Claire and measured out her words, "The first rule of loving somebody like Annabelle is not let her do you harm. She would bring drugs and murder into this house and think nothing of it."

"Sad to say, but I see what you are saying. What do you think, Alexa?" Claire admitted the brutal facts.

"I'm with Thelma. I'd like her to be my mother and live here with us, but we've been visiting her at the prison for years and haven't seen any sign of a kind heart towards me."

"Well, then, what would the halfway house be like?" continued Claire knowing they all wanted to discuss the situation honestly and be prepared for what would happen next.

"As far as I know, there will be other released criminal women, giving them a place to stay and some supervision. I don't really think it will change her, but it will give her shelter. Got any other ideas?"

"What if she went to a totally different part of the country where she didn't know the drug people. Would that give her a new start?" offered Claire.

"Then if she got into trouble, we might not be able to help her," observed Thelma, revealing her softer side. "The halfway house and a whole lot of prayers are the best we can do for now, I think," said Thelma. "This isn't going to be easy, but we have thirty days to think about it, so let's not worry now. Pray for no harm and something good," summarized Thelma.

"Agreed," said Claire and Alexa, taking a moment of silence before clearing the table and cleaning up the kitchen.

"By the way, I have the month's rent for you, Thelma. The job at the bakery is working out really well," offered Claire, pulling out some cash from her jeans pocket.

"Thanks," said Thelma counting the money to estimate how it would be apportioned to cover all of their needs. Her car needed new tires and taxes would be due soon. "Thanks, this helps me a lot."

"Also, I heard from my brother Ernie. He said he's glad I've moved in with you and says that he will come for a visit around Christmas."

"He'll be welcome," promised Thelma.

"Tell him to bring his guitar. I love his music," said Alexa.

The look on Thelma's face was appreciation for the income representing a small lifting of the burdens of her life. Claire thought how good always comes in little packages, gradually over time. First one person helps another and then that one helps a third. Claire had always believed that, but she had not fully appreciated the part about not letting another with poor intentions do harm to her. She resolved to always pray for no harm and lots of good. She thought about her husband and decided to thank him for all the good things he'd done for her.

With that, they all retired to the living room to watch Alexa's latest DVD on old monuments in Peru. They thoroughly enjoyed the film, watching her enthusiasm and asking many questions. Together they wondered about the ancient mysteries, which might still have relevance today. Alexa pointed out some of the symbols in the wall carvings, explaining what she thought they meant, a special talent of hers. As she spoke, the characteristics of the culture and their intentions became clear. If people do have prior lives, surely Alexa had lived in Peru and Egypt and knew their cultures well. With such interest, Alexa would make a fine archeologist and Claire and Thelma intended to help her reach that goal.

Retiring for bed, Claire took a moment to sit at her window looking at the stars. She thought about the ancient peoples who looked at the same stars and perhaps thought the same thoughts as she. Again, the quiet moment slowed her sense of time and she mentally created images of ancient peoples around campfires. But soon, she yawned and slipped into bed, later dreaming of Peruvian people with feathers on their heads and ear bobs in their ear lobes, drawing symbols in the sand after looking at the stars in bowls of water. They turned to her looking surprised she had arrived to visit with them. Since ancient people lived in conscious contact with their souls, Claire could now understand how they must have felt. And so she slept recalling other cultures and times in the company of people looking at the stars, which served all humanity as mirrors to the great mysteries of the universe.

Chapter 10:
The Blessings of Peace

Would it seem silly for a beauty queen to state her mission in life to be Peace on Earth? Would everyone say, "Oh, yeah, but. . ."? Many say trusting a future so simply defined as peaceful would be naive. As Claire would record in her notebook, peace in itself would prove to be an easy thing for the three roommates to create in their own home and a mighty blessing to both protect the family from harm and also to bring more good than they ever imagined.

For now, it was early in the morning and she struggled through her dreams, trying to awaken. After the dreams of ancient peoples, she had dreamed about President Reagan shaking his finger at the Russians, followed by an image of knives being thrown at a girl twirling round and round on a table top at the circus. Thinking about it later, Claire felt she had been that girl on the twirling table at a few points in her life. In real circuses, the girl willingly climbs on the table, but Claire felt she had little choice about the intentional daggers she had at times faced. Her brother often joked that, in their generation, children were expected to be quiet, behave and be some help, not objecting to what they were told. Ironically, these same children grew up to organize peace rallies and stand together singing

"Give Peace A Chance." She, too, grew up with those long, forgotten conflicting beliefs of childhood needing to be changed by the adult she had become.

The prior night's discussion about not allowing harm had struck a strong chord in her heart. Indeed, a new way for making peace was needed. Although she struggled to wake, she only fell back into deeper sleep, where a much more instructive and enjoyable dream played in her mind. In this dream, she was flying away from a dark cave as a small black bat among many small black bats emerging from the dark. As she flew into the morning light, she became a white stork gracefully flying a long distance away from the dark cave. Circling above the land, she looked for a new place to live, a place suitable for a beautiful white stork. Finally, she found a quiet grove of very tall trees. There she was joined by many other birds like herself and made a nest that would last for a long time.

As this dream was so beautiful, she wanted to stay in it; the sensation of flying was delightful and the quiet grove of trees seemed like a good home to her. She relaxed, but all too soon woke to the alarm announcing 5:30 a.m.

Today was her first art class and she was looking forward to the experience. Over cereal and yogurt, she and Alexa discussed Claire's dreams and the day ahead for each of them. Alexa thought that the Peruvian dream was actually a recall of a past life experience. The others had to do with Claire taking charge of her life by prohibiting anyone from doing her harm. Indeed, she could fly free to find her own home and companions. Claire thanked her, acknowledging the child's skills in dream interpretation, which she had probably gained in some forgotten lifetime. Alexa was pleased and smiled.

After Alexa left on the school bus, Claire pulled out the art class description to review the supply list: a selection of brushes, tubes of acrylic paint in various colors and a set of canvas boards in different sizes. There was also a note to bring a photo of something to paint. Claire had selected an old calendar of country scenes she had saved just because she liked the pictures. Packing all in a carry bag, she felt ready for the class. Cleaning up the kitchen, she decided to complete a few other chores for the house before leaving for the community recreation center.

The art classroom was very large, sunny and filled with long tables, easels and a chalkboard. The other students were men and women near her age or a bit younger; most of them, like Claire, had little or no art training. The teacher, Linda Logan, was tall, slim and cheerful with a competent manner. She quickly introduced the classmates to each other, settled them at tables and began a demonstration of what to do with the canvases and paints. She started her demonstration by painting an entire canvas with a color called Naples Yellow, and then began to create figures and forms based on a selected photo. After the demonstration, most of the class began painting. Some followed the example of the demonstration and others began to copy their own photo section by section.

Claire liked the idea of a whole canvas of Naples Yellow, because it seemed to be such a happy way to start a painting. The color made her think of a sunny Italian village about to emerge from the thick paint, or in the case of her photo, a barn with a tree in front of a pasture. However, once she had the whole canvas covered in the delicious sunny color, she was at a loss as to how to depict her picture of a field of hay, tree and barn. She sat and thought for a few minutes, which brought Linda over to suggest using a wide flat brush with some dark brown paint to create the general form of the barn. Squirting some brown paint beside the yellow, Claire dipped the brush in both, making a warm tone of brown with streaks of yellow. She applied the broad strokes with a steady hand. The paint flowed in multiple tones across the roof of the barn and then with more paint applied, the sides of the barn took shape. She was delighted with the effects of the wide flat brush.

Admiring the barely started painting as if it were a masterful completion, Claire heard the thoughts of her Soul Self suggest, *Why not use the same colors and brush to do the tree?*

Claire started with the tree trunk intending to go up, but soon found the brush was too wide to make the branches. She selected a narrower one for the branches. That worked so well, she had to once again admire her work. Linda returned again, suggesting a basic shade of green mixed with the yellow to make masses of leaves on the tree.

Claire searched through her brushes and found a round thick brush that would hold a lot of paint. Loading it with the green and yellow, she dabbed blotches of colors that seemed to mix themselves on the canvas. Surprisingly, the blotches looked like masses of leaves. She was surprised at how well the suggestions were working. So it was with confidence that Claire saw how she could finish the painting by adding more detail made from slightly darker or lighter shades of the same colors. Actually, she only used a few colors for the whole painting. Fully engrossed in comparing the details of the photo to the canvas, she heard the thought from Soul Self, *You are making a beautiful home where I can live, so paint a few birds to be my family in the branches of the tree.*

She wondered about the implication that her Soul Self would live in the painting. The thought reminded her about her dream of being a white bird. Since she didn't know how to paint birds, she asked Linda, who suggested a simple wavy line for the wings and a thicker line for the body. It was only a suggestion of birds, but it worked well.

How's that? she thought.

How's a bird going to eat if there isn't a pond with insects and lots of wildflowers making seeds? her Soul Self queried.

Oh, well, if you insist. I'll use a little blue to make a pond to the right of the barn and put in weeds, flowers and insects. There, how do you like it? Claire laughed to herself about creating a place for insects and decided the pond wouldn't produce enough of them to feed a good flock of birds, so she added the impressions of a herd of brown cows in the distant Naples yellow field of hay. *There, lots of cows and manure! That should keep you from getting hungry, my little bird friends.* She smiled as she realized she was having fun, as if the Soul Self were a person standing beside her like a teacher, helping her with the painting. Having now grown used to the comforting conversations with her Soul Self, it was a great pleasure to her to listen for the friendly and helpful thoughts. During these conversations, she couldn't talk or even listen to others. Focusing only on her work, her thoughts and the conversations with her Soul Self, it all blended within her into a single enjoyable flow of emotion. It was a joyful experience that was there for her anytime.

All too soon, Linda concluded class with a few words about art as a form of communication:

"As an artist, you can create an image of an experience you're having so the viewers can also experience what you saw and felt. You are portraying your own world and the viewers get to live there with you for a few moments of enjoyment."

Claire was stunned by the thought of someone else living in the world she had depicted in her painting. She compared what the teacher had said to the thought of her Soul Self living in the painting as a bird in the tree. She wondered why anyone would want to spend time looking at her primitive first painting, but if so, what would they know about her and what would she know about them? Would they feel the joy she felt?

She was the last to leave the classroom and thanked the teacher for her words and her help, promising to return in the fall. The canvas was almost dry, but she carried it carefully to her car and laid it flat in the trunk. She planned to place it on the kitchen table so Thelma and Alexa could see it and say what they thought. She'd made a good decision to sign up for the free art class and she certainly had the option to paint during the summer on her own and then sign up for many more classes. What a difference between yesterday and today, or rather what a progression from the fears of depression to the peaceful art class. She hoped the rest of her life would be like that, happy.

At supper, Thelma and Alexa carefully looked at the painting, walking their thoughts through the barn, sitting under the tree and walking through the cow field.

"When I was a child, I lived near a cow field where I would walk," recalled Thelma. "It was filled with insects, weeds, manure and, of course, big cows that stood and stared at me. I loved those days."

"Aunt Claire, I had no idea you could paint so well. Will you teach me how?" queried Alexa.

"I've never painted before in my life. To tell you the truth, the teacher and Soul Self talked me through the painting. The time went so fast and I completely enjoyed it. I'll teach you what I know. It'll be fun."

As the evening progressed from one topic to the next, Thelma told stories of the elderly people in the nursing home where she worked as a cook and sandwich maker in the deli.

Harold, who suffered from dementia and only rarely knew where he was, came to the deli thinking Thelma was his sweetheart from years gone by. He asked her out for a date. Having been trained to play along with the illusions of dementia as long as it did no harm, Thelma responded:

"Who me? Are you talking to me? You want me to go out on a date with you?"

Harold responded, "Yes, don't you remember I asked you out before?"

"Well, yes," Thelma said, fluffing her hair in mock disdain, "but look at you. You still have your pajamas and robe on. Do you expect me to go out with you dressed like that? Here's your sandwich. Have a seat and eat your lunch and I'll let you know later."

Harold laughed vigorously. *How could he have overlooked the fact he had his pajamas on?* He often wondered why he wore them so much and why there was an elevator in his house and so many people. About that time, Thelma came over to his table singing a boogie-woogie song and bringing his drink.

"Hey handsome soldier, want my number?" she asked with a racy tone. Again he laughed, remembering the old music and his wartime service. Each time he laughed, his mind cleared a little. Suddenly he saw Thelma as she really was, a worker in the deli and said to her, "Don't flirt with me, I'm a married man!" At this point, Thelma turned to leave with the retort, "Why are the good ones always married?" They both laughed and Thelma went on with her work and Harold with his memories.

This was daily life in a nursing home, and Thelma never tired of it. She found the residents' long and old stories very interesting and she, of course, loved to joke about anything, even an illusion. When all else failed, a good old song would make the day a bright one. Retelling the incidents over the supper table only added to the fun and Claire and Alexa got to know the nursing home residents well by virtue of the stories.

After such a nice meal and accompanying stories, they all decided to take their bowels of ice cream and sit on the porch to look at the new moon rising and it's companion stars. The threesome felt such moments of peace, rest and gentle conversation to be precious to their sanity. Nothing was too small to mention or too unimportant to earn a comment. With such small tendrils of mutual caring such as these, families are made strong, and within thirty days, that strength of family would be tested and found to be highly resilient. But for now, it was just a pleasure.

Claire's thoughts strayed to her plans for the week. Tomorrow was a workday at the bakery and her first counseling appointment had been rescheduled after work due to her art class on Monday. As well, Claire thought she and Alexa should go to the library some afternoon this week to get photo books from which to paint. She was beginning to realize she needed to look more closely at things to see the light and shadows, which a painter uses to make things look real on canvas. Little did she know, but she had gained some critical insights into the world of art and had set herself on a path to learn more and more. She had set the intention to enjoy learning to paint and thus it was, just as she intended.

Wanting to take a few moments to write in her notebook, she said goodnight to the porch sitters and climbed the stairs to her apartment. As she opened the most recent notes, she thought about how lovingly Soul Self had guided her with wise and valuable advice. Just the few notes in the notebook had helped her to feel safe from harm and to be able to prosper in new endeavors. With confidence, she decided to inquire about the dream of the night before.

Claire: Soul Self, I wish to thank you for the love and good advice you've given me. For the first time since my parents died, I feel safe and loved. Thank you. I had the dream about President Reagan and the bats and the birds. Would you share with me what they meant?

Soul Self: You are most welcome! Please realize that I am the parent of your growing human mind and I am forever responsible for you. I love and care for you because you are my child.

Claire: I never thought of it that way before. So you are the reason I am here. I came from you. I thought God created everything.

Soul Self: Indeed and then God said, "Go forth and multiply," so we did. That's how you came to be living in my aura womb.

Claire: That's beautiful. I never saw it that way before. So we are all one big family.

Soul Self: God is all about family, love and peace. It couldn't be any other way. Jesus told people of his day the same thing when he told stories of families and referred to his Father in heaven.

Claire: It's so simple, loving and familiar. Wow!

Soul Self: Indeed! Now, let me explain your dream.

The formative intention for this sharing of thoughts, which you call a dream, was your request to never be harmed. Was that not what President Reagan was doing by threatening retaliation if harm was initiated by another country? The threats and counter threats were designed to prevent harm during the Cold War, a methodology of trusting the untrustworthy, which satisfied the need to show strength as well as restraint. Therefore, in this dream, you and I were thinking about this time in history and giving thanks it served a peaceful purpose. However, in the end, we recognized how stressful it was for everyone and wanted a new way to find peace.

The dream about the girl having knives thrown at her while whirling around on a tabletop depicted the stress and anxiety you've lived through believing yourself helpless to stop people from harming you. Many women of your generation feel the same way. I want you to know no blade ever struck you, but even more, you don't have to live this way. You are reviewing these old fears so as to let them go. How can you be happy when you are afraid. . .about anything?

Indeed, the dream about the bat and the stork implied you are not a blind bat living in a dark hole of fear. Because you declared you want to be happy, you see yourself as you really are, a beautiful white bird of good fortune free to go wherever you want. And you wanted a new place to be yourself, free of the dark expectations of your generation. Wanting freedom is one of the first steps toward happiness. As you flew over the landscape in the dream, you only wanted a quiet place to make a home and raise new expectations for yourself in the company of those of like mind. It was a great dream, don't you think?

Claire: Yes, I can see that. But what is my new home? I like it here at Thelma's.

Soul Self: It's just like Thelma's home. It's the home of your expectations for yourself, essentially to be safe, content, productive and happy.

114

Claire: Yes, that's what I want! I want to be safe, content, productive and happy. That's all I've ever wanted. Has it taken me this long to recognize that? It's only now I think I can have that without interference. What's made the difference?

Soul Self: Could we have had this discussion without the death of a marriage, the depression or the vivid dreams? You were always on the perfect path to achieve happiness, every step of the way. It just took some turning experiences to understand it all. Rejoice and be glad you've arrived. Nothing was ever wrong, just not fully arrived until now.

Claire: Hmm. So this is how you helped me to see my whole life and all of my experiences as happy, on the road to being happier yet. The only way I can be happy is to be happy with my past. By the way, thanks for the art class.

Soul Self: Piece of cake. You are welcome. May I take the time to drastically change the subject and suggest you find a new dentist in the area? There is need for you to continue having dental care every six months without fail so you can be happy. Agreed?

Claire: Yes, certainly so. Thanks for looking after me to assure my happiness. That's true friendship and love, more to the point, parental love.

Soul Self: Thanks for being there with me when I wanted to be a bird living by that peaceful barn you painted. Together we painted a picture of our new happy pasture of expectations. We can live in those fertile expectations together in peace. After all, where you go, I go, so let's make it a good place to be happy.

Claire: I will never go anywhere without you, my friend. Goodnight!

No amount of attitude adjustment could have created such a moment of contented peace for Claire. Her decision to be happy was being played out in real life. It was not just wishful thinking that she had a secure and happy home, good medical care, a better job and a new creative interest. All together it was proof a well-founded intention for good does not fail.

Claire closed the notebook, made ready for bed and relaxed under the covers, looking out the window. The stars twinkled brightly through the window in a dark sky lit by the moon and the crickets sang for hours while the dew formed on the grass. All things on earth were a vast family wanting to live in peace, for only peace can give freedom, which inevitably produces joy. All things had the order of the universe to guide them and they were all doing what they needed to do to be present at their own magic moment of joy. It was indeed a good night for the intention for The Highest Good to be lived out in peace.

Chapter 11:
Great Expectations

What is a great expectation but an opportunity to be happy three times over, once in the making of the intention, twice in the spending of the time having it happen and third in the remembrance? On this day of great expectations, Claire held true to her original intention to be happy with no specifics in mind. She had learned to enjoy this most simple intention because it made happiness come in so many different, but related forms, unfolding into mysteriously beautiful days.

Arriving at the bakery the next day, the now familiar routines and teamwork at the bakery required her complete attention. First to arrive at the shop was Ed, who was always the first, mainly because he lived in the apartment upstairs. As usual, he had turned on the lights and started the ovens, setting up the equipment and coffeemakers in preparation for Claire's arrival. As she put on her apron and assembled the ingredients to make her bread dough, he began to talk to her.

"I remember when I worked at the boxboard plant. There was always some things only the first person in the department could do. I was the supervisor for a while and I had to turn on the machines and change the cutting blades. When the other workers arrived, things were ready to go."

"I sure appreciate you doing all of this for me. Did you like being a supervisor?" asked Claire absently as she carefully measured and mixed ingredients.

"Yes, at first, but later there were so many problems with people not getting to work on time and not doing what I told them to do, it got to be pretty difficult," mused Ed. "I promised myself that I'd never be a supervisor again and I won't."

"Too bad," said Claire, "you would be a good supervisor. I've only had one supervisor I ever respected or liked. When I was young, I waited tables in a restaurant and the supervisor was wonderful to work for. We never had any trouble. Everybody got their work done and made their tips."

"That's what I wanted to be like, but I could never figure out how to do it," replied Ed, with his dark eyes sparkling, as he helped Claire lift the large bowl into the giant mixer. "Want to do the other one next?"

"No, today's orders are smaller than yesterday's. I think I'll just make the one mixer today. Oh, look, there's Gwen."

Gwen Yardley entered her shop, quickly looking around to see what needed to be done. She was the boss who was never bossy, the supervisor who never had to say anything twice. She checked that each employee could and would do their job and then let them do it. When the employees had fully learned their jobs, they were encouraged to improve a little bit everyday and she would gladly help them. It was both her nature and her heritage.

Gwen, a tall, slender black woman with neat curly hair, had been born in Cincinnati as a descendent of one of the many families who fled the South during the Civil War. These former slaves settled in Cincinnati where jobs were plentiful and people were open to training the black refugees in the skills needed to make the city a commercial powerhouse of skilled tradespeople and retail merchants. Gwen was the fifth generation of these skilled refugees and she had learned her bakery craft from childhood. Having been happily married a long time, but without children, her husband had passed away fifteen years earlier. After his death, she devoted herself to her business and the people in the community in which the bakery flourished. A naturally kind and respectful person, Gwen talked to each person individually and solved the problems of the moment, ignoring all complaints and excuses in favor of a positive attitude. She had found peace in her life and saw each day as a blessing. It was a simple philosophy, but it worked to make the bakery a pleasant and productive place to work among friends.

The only other employee on the weekday shift, was Mrs. Greene, who arrived with a plump smile and specific plans in mind for all she had to do that day. She was about as wide as she was tall and wrapped her white apron around her waistless frame using long ties. With her tight grey hair and tiny blue eyes, Mrs. Greene came originally from England, where she and her husband had owned and operated a pastry shop in Brighton. Having immigrated to America, they wanted to find a place to open a new and better bakery. At first, they settled in Boston where their shop had prospered for many years until her husband died from lung cancer. When she decided she did not have the heart to continue the business, she sold it to the highest bidder. Traveling to the Midwest looking for employment, she knew she'd have to work for someone she trusted and by whom she would be treated as family. That was Gwen for sure. Gwen let her make her pastries the way she liked as long as the customers were enthusiastic. Never had Mrs. Greene found so much appreciation for her craft and friendliness with so few hassles and worries. Indeed, the customers and employees were like a family and she happily took the role of queen of the pastry case, ruling with her high standards, British accent, humor and experience.

With the bakery staff complete, the prep work progressed rapidly and soon the shop was open and ready for business. The first customers were always the same. Mr. and Mrs. Clooney brought their newspapers to read while sipping coffee with still-warm pastries. Each read completely different newspapers and never discussed news or politics between themselves, thereby sharing their pastries and their days in contentment.

"Good morning, Mrs. Greene," said Mr. Clooney. "What have you for us today?"

"You have to try this raspberry and nut Danish, which even the Danish can't make right," said Mrs. Greene in her best British accent. "But also, I have a new pastry I am keeping secret, which has oranges and pumpkin seeds. I had to send away for just the right blend of nuts and cinnamon, and then I added a snip of ginger. When I've perfected them, I will put them out, but you can have a preview." Knowing better than to ask what a snip of ginger was, Mr. Clooney smiled and soberly agreed that he and his wife would be honored to be taste testers for the new pumpkin seed pastries. Mrs. Greene nodded as if she were a conductor of an orchestra who turned and bowed to the audience to be applauded as would be expected.

"Give us one of each and Mrs. Clooney will also have one of the lemon butter cakes for a late lunch she's having with her friends," requested Mr. Clooney. "Dear, could you get us the coffee?" he addressed his wife formally as he always did, even though she was already getting their coffee made just the way they liked. The couple then settled at their same favorite sunny table and unfolded their newspapers.

Next came the young mothers who, after dropping off their children at day care and school, stopped for coffee and donuts before heading off to work. Several had come to the shop as little girls, growing up in the little community of families who patronized the bakery. They had known each other as teenagers, single women and now mothers. They chatted about their children, their jobs and their homes while they waited to be served, then off they went to their busy days.

About midday, someone new came in. An older man with a sad face ordered a coffee and a Danish. He then sat at a table by himself, looking out the window. Immediately, Gwen went over to him.

"Hello, my name is Gwen. I own the shop, may I sit down?"

"Of course, I'm Mike Adams," his face brightened.

"How did you find the bakery?" Gwen asked pleasantly.

"I was early for my doctor's appointment and I saw your sign. Since the shop was busy, I decided to give it a try," replied Mike.

"I hope you like the pastry and coffee, but you might also try our breads. Claire is just about to put fresh loaves warm from the oven in the case."

"Oh, I would like that," said Mike brightening still more. "My mother used to make bread at home and gave us some when we got home from school."

Gwen rose and asked Claire to prepare a slice of fresh bread to bring to Mike. When Claire brought the sample to his table, he took a big bite and asked, "So what do you put into this bread to get this particular flavor and crust?"

Claire replied, "The herbs are rosemary and dill, but the rest is my secret. Would you like to try it with butter?"

"I was thinking of cream cheese. I have to keep my cholesterol down, you know."

"Well, you've come to the wrong place for that. I might suggest fresh strawberries with no butter *or* cream cheese would work well. Are you just watching the cholesterol or is it watching you?"

"I'm afraid I've already lost the game on that score. I've had one heart attack already and, according to my doctor, I'm likely to have another."

"I'm sorry to hear that."

"I'm participating in an experimental medicine trial, which means I have to be tested once a week. It's a hassle, but my doctor has high hopes the drug will work."

"I'm glad we were on your way. Would you like to take a sample for your doctor to try?"

Mike laughed. " Do you stop at nothing to make friends with bread dough?"

Claire laughed as well. "If you can laugh, you can live, my father always said and I believe him."

"Well, if you put it that way, give me a sample and I'll be off to see the doctor."

Claire packaged a sample of bread and rang up Mike's bill, which he paid in cash. As she gave him his change, their hands touched for a moment and a spark of static jumped between them. They both drew back. There was a pause long enough and the senses strong enough for both to take in a quick breath, and then to look aside to go on as if nothing had happened.

Mike pocketed his change and left. Turning away from the cash register for the kitchen, Claire once again saw things in a very clear and motionless way, just as she had the day of her doctor's appointment. She felt she was an observer of some other self just like her, but separate. She savored the moment as she had before, but she knew something had happened to change her life that could not be reversed.

Claire went back into the kitchen not just to clean up some dishes, but also to take a moment to listen to her Soul Self who said, *Be not afraid. When a kindness passes between two people, they often open to their higher minds, sending great amounts of loving energy between each other*. She smiled to herself, knowing she had felt kindness and appreciation between her and Mike. She decided it was just a momentary thing, despite the fact her hands were still shaking.

Later the district librarian, Lillian, came in to remind everyone about the used book sale this week. As a fundraiser, the library asked for donations of used books from the community and then organized them to be resold at the book sale. This reminded Claire she wanted to take Alexa to the library to look for picture books with good photos to paint.

In addition to the librarian, the mother of one of their regular customers came in looking for something for breakfast the next morning for her grandchildren. Indulging in such sweets was not her habit, but her grandchildren were staying overnight and she wanted something special. After a long discussion with Mrs. Greene, the grandmother decided on a dozen cookies with sprinkles on them. Admittedly, she would never have let her own children have cookies for breakfast, but grandchildren were something else. After she left, everyone smiled, knowing they would hear more of this story before the week was out.

Finally, it was time for Claire to leave for her first counseling appointment. She folded her apron to take it home to be washed, saying goodbye to all. At the medical services building, she found the counseling offices, where Scott called her from the waiting room. She was a bit nervous, but was glad to see him again.

Scott showed her to his office and greeted her in a friendly manner. "Hello, Claire, have a seat. Let me pull up my notes on the computer and we'll get started. I remember we were going to start with getting better acquainted with you and your history. Are you comfortable with that? Do you have any questions?"

"Well, I always wondered, just what is depression anyhow?"

Scott replied, "Freud said depression is anger turned inward. But mental health professionals today look at it as the inability to function well on a daily basis that may have many different causes including generalized stress. One of our goals is to determine if your depression is caused by longstanding emotions resulting from life situations such as you have had or other factors. Does that give you something of an answer to your question?"

"I guess so. I admit I'm not functioning very well and at times, I feel very upset about a lot of things."

"This is an excellent place to start. Let's take a baseline measurement of how well you are functioning now and how well you'd like to be functioning. I remember you said you want to be happy. So on a scale of one to ten, how happy and functional do you think you are now?" Scott was proving to be very methodical, which was comforting to Claire.

"About a five. I have taken steps to resolve all of the financial problems, but the hearing has not taken place yet and the debts have left me homeless. My friend Thelma gave me an apartment in her duplex for the time being in exchange for helping her with her granddaughter, Alexa. But I still feel sad and worried about things. And yes, I feel angry that so much in my life has been uprooted. I feel like I have lost everything!" replied Claire, sadly. "I miss my husband and the life that we had, but honestly, I have to admit it was not the best marriage."

"I see. Take a minute to feel those feelings. They are very normal and natural for the situation and they will come and go over and over again, I'm sure." Scott waited for a minute, taking notes. Then he continued, "Let's start with the first thing you mentioned. You said you'd taken some steps to resolve the financial problems. Would you describe them and discuss how satisfied you are with them?"

Claire once again looked at the sad outcome of her life and summarized, " After my husband died, I had huge medical bills, so I found an attorney and she said to sell the house and she'd try to negotiate the rest of the bills for the difference. She said I would still have good credit and no debts, but no home. That's how I wound up living with Thelma and Alexa. I hated to give up my home, but I did. There will be a hearing soon to resolve it all."

Scott decided to focus on her current situation. "A good start. How do you like living with Thelma and Alexa?"

"Actually, I love it. They are like my family and I want to pay monthly rent, which would help Thelma a lot. I guess I am free of obligations of a house and a husband at this point, but I just don't have anything, but a part-time job.

"Where do you work? Do you like being there?"

"I had a job doing bookkeeping, but I lost that, so I started making bread and selling it at the farmer's market. Then the owner of a local bakery asked me if I wanted a part-time job, so I work there now and I like it."

"It sounds like you have made good progress dealing with some very difficult problems. You should be proud of what you have accomplished, even if there is a lot more that you want for yourself." Scott wanted to emphasize Claire's progress, sensing she lacked confidence in herself.

"I try to think about it that way," Claire sighed. "Most of the time, I feel like a disaster area."

"Most of what we think about ourselves is distorted by strong emotions. Your feelings of loss give you the perception you are a disaster. That is what depression is all about. You think you are a disaster because you feel so bad, but actually you have done some good things for yourself despite a difficult situation." Claire would undoubtedly think about that point and Scott would refer to it later. In the meantime, he waited to see what she would say.

After a pause, Claire looked at him wondering how much she could tell him about her conversations with the Soul Self. She decided to edge around the topic cautiously. "Do you believe that bad things happen just by luck, or that there is a reason for them?"

Perceiving that she wanted some reassurance she was not responsible for these bad events in her life, Scott responded by saying, "Bad things happen to people for whatever reason, but everyone can choose how to respond. You have chosen to respond well. If you hadn't made good choices for yourself, your problems would be worse and the strong emotions of grief would continue for a long time, determining your future. Is that what you were asking?"

"Sort of. A good friend told me to set a goal of being happy and to have no doubt that I wanted it. My friend said it was a matter of cooperation," she disguised her conversations with Soul Self and watching to see Scott's reaction.

"Good advice, I'd say. It fits your situation very well. So how has it worked for you?"

"Very well, if I could just shake these sad feelings," Claire replied, surprised to have come to this conclusion by herself and to have it approved by someone who knows how these things go. "But I wouldn't say that I am completely happy all of the time."

"Yes, the feelings are strong and will continue for a while, but if you continue to want to improve, they will gradually diminish. If you want some medications, the doctor can prescribe them." Scott made a few notes on the computer.

"No, I don't want any medications. All I want is for the bad things to stop happening and to stay at Thelma's house for awhile," said Claire, sliding down into her chair.

"Well, let's go with that for now. Just to complete my notes, let's look at your family history and other members of your support system. Where did you grow up? Tell me about your family and childhood." Scott went back to his methodical note taking.

Claire began a summary of her childhood. "My parents raised my brother and I in Cincinnati with a religious education.

My mother didn't work, staying home to take care of us. My dad made a good living as a manager of a service company. Actually, we were a good family and Mom and Dad taught us to save money, work hard and go to church. They died years ago. My brother Ernie helped me with my husband's funeral and is going to go with me to the last debt settlement hearing."

"So Ernie is a big part of your support system along with Thelma and Alexa," pointed out Scott. "Anyone else?"

Again, Claire hesitated, unsure if she should mention Soul Self, but she asked, "Do you believe in people being psychic?"

"Yes. Does that mean something to you?"

"Well, Thelma is psychic and does readings for people. She hears from people who have passed over. Do you think that means she's crazy?"

"Not necessarily. Are you asking about people who hear voices and are mentally ill?" smiled Scott.

"Yes, I do want to know that."

"There are mental illnesses in which people hear voices in their heads, telling them to do harmful things or make unrealistic claims. They can be diagnosed and treated." It was Scott's turn to wonder if Claire was hearing voices. "Do you want to talk about that?"

"What if I were making bread and got some wonderful ideas I never thought of before and the bread turned out to be great, then I got more and more good ideas. Where would these ideas come from?"

"I'd think you are referring to intuition, which is a normal part of being human. Many people such as inventors and artists highly value their intuition. Do you experience that?"

"Yes, I do. It is very clear and I can ask questions and get answers that are very good. What do you think about that?" Claire was gaining confidence.

"I'd say it was a good thing. It does not sound crazy. But if you'd like a referral to a psychiatrist for an evaluation, I can arrange for that." Scott was following standard procedure, but was not alarmed at what Claire had said.

"No, I'm not worried I'm crazy, but it does sound strange. Outside of Thelma, I don't know anybody else who talks about this sort of thing." Claire was relieved to be able to talk about this, even though she had been convinced from the beginning it was a good thing.

"You said you had a strong religious education and such experiences might be part of your faith, but I assure you everybody has intuition. Claire, let's make a pact. If you tell me honestly what's going on with you, I'll tell you if I hear anything crazy that needs attention. Deal?"

"Deal!"

"Well, our time is up. Thanks for being such a good client and I will see you next week. I will keep Dr. Connor informed of my notes," Scott said concluding the session.

"OK, thanks. See you next week." Claire walked out relieved to have Scott as a counselor.

She proceeded home in time to greet Alexa and Cassie getting off of the bus. "Hi, girls. How was your day?"

Both replied by detailing the latest assignment in science class and who liked who, with or without success. Then Cassie left for her house with a wave and Claire and Alexa settled in the kitchen for a snack and talked.

"I thought I'd go to the library book sale to find some books of photos for ideas of what to paint," Claire said. "Want to go?"

Alexa nodded yes, but also eyed her carefully. "Aunt Claire, you look different somehow. What happened today?"

Claire privately debated about telling anyone about the mysterious touch of two hands between her and Mike, but Alexa was so innocent, honest and wise, Claire told her all about the conversation and the moments of still happiness that followed. She ended with the comment from her Soul Self about the energy that flows between two people when there has been a kindness given and appreciated.

" Are you talking about love? Aunt Claire, are you falling in love with this man?" Alexa asked with characteristic family bluntness. Indeed at her age, she should not know about such things, but she did. Claire had noticed at times she seemed no longer a child, rather she spoke as a wise old soul.

"Well, it's not like falling in love. It's more like . . . " Claire could not finish the sentence and both thought for a few moments in silence while munching cookies. Finally, Alexa said, "I remember a line from a poem, 'To be silent must be love because love has no name, it only has feeling.'"

Again there was a long silence with nothing further to be said. Soon after, they proceeded to the library book sale. There, they found rows and rows of books, some used and some appearing new. Claire went to the photo books and Alexa went to the history and archeology books. Both were entirely engrossed in their selections when Claire finally noticed the time was late. She called for Alexa to come so they could check out and get home before Thelma arrived. Twenty dollars later they were both proud owners of exactly what they wanted and then some.

Spread out on the living room coffee table, the books gave the impression of having been bought at two different sales. Alexa's stack revealed her passion for ancient statues, temples, mummies and artifacts, while Claire's reflected her desire to paint landscapes, gardens and mountains with streams. When Thelma arrived, they were still silently occupied with turning pages. She looked at them with a smile. "Supper will be ready in an hour, if you care to join me."

At the supper table, Thelma asked Claire about the counseling appointment.

"He said I'm not crazy, but I'm depressed. But I liked him and I think it will help."

"I could have told you that. What else?"

Alexa sat forward and took the opportunity to spill the story of Claire's conversation with Mike.

"Aunt Claire met a man at the bakery today. I think they like each other," started Alexa.

"Well, he stopped on his way to the doctor," continued Claire still unsure of just how much she wanted to talk about it. "We chatted over a sample of my bread. When I gave him change, sparks jumped between us. It was just static electricity. It doesn't mean a thing."

"How did it feel later?" asked Thelma with characteristic accuracy.

"Well, actually I had another experience of time standing still, like the day I came home from the doctor's office. It was sort of blissful. But since it had happened before, I don't think it was because of him," said Claire, attempting to downplay the incident.

Thelma looked up at the ceiling as if she were smoking a cigarette, which she wasn't, and blew instead a chimney of thought. Then she said, "Things happen. Don't worry, it is a good thing." Claire relaxed and the discussion changed lanes several times heading first to the topic of history and later to that of photos. What a group of lovers they were! Each loved something of interest and they all loved each other. No one wanted a minute of it to end.

Alone, in her bedroom later that evening, Claire added a few notes to her notebook about the incident.

Claire: Soul Self, you saw what happened today. Why did I get so shaky just to talk to a man about his heart attack?

Soul Self: Have you ever wondered how people felt when Jesus healed them? Their hearts opened to his kindness and they were filled with appreciation. Indeed their hands shook.

Claire: Oh, I never thought about that.

Soul Self: When two people give kindness to each other, the feeling of the Presence of God just flows and that is what you felt.

Claire: The Presence of God???

Soul Self: Where were we when you stopped reading in the little book that no one can understand? Do you remember the part about the souls being made out of God and that God is love? Who do you suppose gave you the urge to show the man such kindness, but me? Who do you suppose gave Mike the appreciation for the kindness and the desire to return it, but his Soul Self? And where do we Soul Selves get the flow of love, but from God?

In all cases of the giving and receiving of kindness, there are Soul Selves at work. We give the urge to be kind and we give the feeling of love. We always do so whenever the human mind allows us the opportunity. There's nothing else we *can* do. Of course, you have the choice to cooperate or not. So what do you think?

Claire: I think it might not be as dangerous to love somebody as I've been thinking. Souls are involved who can't do any harm and they have vast amounts of power to make good things happen. Did I just say that? I thought I was way too scared to love again.

Soul Self: Apparently something has changed, but let's take it a step further. If everybody realized what love was and where it came from, wouldn't they consult with their Soul Selves whenever they needed to be loved or even wanted some company?

Claire: Well, that's what I did and look what happened.

Soul Self: So what do you think will happen next?

Claire: Well, I am still a *bit* apprehensive. I don't want to have any stress in my life. I've had too much of a setback for now and a new relationship would just mean more problems for me, especially someone who could die at any moment. Do I sound negative?

Soul Self: Then ask for a kind friend. The feeling of love is universally available, it's not just for people who fall in love or are married.

Claire: Well, that sounds much better. I'd like to be friends with Mike. He probably has enough on his plate with his health problems, he wouldn't want anything more either. OK, I feel better now. I intend to be friends with this man and many others who appreciate and respect kindness. Yes, that feels good to me. Those moments of the Presence of God are amazing. It's like extreme happiness slowed down. Can I have more of this?

Soul Self: Of course, it is your nature to do so. In fact, you are doing so well that maybe you don't need to read the rest of the book after all.

Claire: I think eventually, I'll read it all. It does have a way of making me think differently about life. Maybe that's what takes so long to understand. People need to live it to understand it.

Soul Self: Well said. That's all I have to say about that.

Claire: How about good night after a good day? How about thank you and I love you? Claire crossed her fingers over her heart.

Soul Self: Ditto.

Claire closed her notebook with a smile and made ready for bed. As she slipped between the covers, she wondered about the good things ahead for her to experience. In saying she wanted to be happy, she had set a great expectation, but had no specific ideas about what would happen, and then found even her wildest dreams were exceeded. Her eyes closed and she slipped into sleep, the kind of sleep children have when they know they are loved and their parents are looking after them. This watchful spirit parent, however, was everywhere and in each moment forever. Indeed something had changed in the bakery that could and should not be reversed, but it wasn't just two people. It was much bigger than that.

Chapter 12:
The Story Unfolds

When one chapter ends, then another picks up the line of the story and continues on until the reader closes the book and selects another. Isn't that what every novelist likes to portray and every reader to enjoy? Why live just one life when many would do? To do so in a novel is safe and easy, but what if a graceful insight spills off the page into the reader's own life? Would such an experience change everything? Is that what makes a masterpiece so special, whether a story, a statue or a painting? Would it be the same spark of kindness followed by joy that Claire and Mike experienced, only much more?

Claire's time off from work constituted private time to do what she wanted and enjoy herself without interruption. Such an opportunity was delicious and she was determined that nothing but enjoyment be allowed. She wanted no silent slander of herself about something she should have done or didn't do, no pursuit of a goal or a task to accomplish constituting success or failure. She had no one to report to, take care of or provide for. This was her time for herself. *How wonderful*, she thought.

Alexa having left for school that day, Claire set about a light cleaning of Thelma's kitchen and her own apartment upstairs.

She liked things to be clean and in order, but not excessively so. With that done, she wanted the pleasure of writing in her notebook. She settled at her table and chair in front of the window and began to write.

Claire: I've been content the past few days. It's a good feeling, and I don't know when I've felt this way before, maybe not for a very long a time.

Soul Self: Me, too. I have felt very content as well. You have become so cooperative with our work together, it's been no effort at all making good things happen for you. It just seems to flow. Did you notice the beautiful sunrise this morning? I selected the colors just for you to notice. Would you like to paint it on canvas today?

Claire: Yes, I did notice it. It was a beautiful mixture of gold and orange rising into the blue. What did you mean you selected the colors just for me? Didn't the rest of the world see the same sunrise?

Soul Self: Some yes and some no. Some saw it as the sign of a new day but ignored its beauty. Others never saw it in the first place. But there are always a few who have to stop and admire the artwork of a sunrise and feel appreciation. They are the ones who experience the spark of joy. You are such a one.

Claire: Oh, I see what you mean. I know that spark of joy. You mentioned how things can sometimes just flow. I always wondered about the phrase *Go with the flow*. Would you say more about that?

Soul Self: When one has a good time, one never needs to ask what time it is or when does it come to an end. Time is meaningless. Much like the slow-motion moments of joy you've experienced, happiness intensifies itself and slows down your perception of time. And then it unfolds like a flower. It does not just go on. You have to go into it, not just go on with it. You've noticed you have to slow down and look to find joy. It's not on the road to somewhere else. It's right here, right now. Want to give it a try now?

Claire: Sure. I would love it.

Soul Self: It'll be easy. Get out your canvas and paints, open the tube of your favorite Naples Yellow and put a glob of it on your palette. Just look at the color and relax into enjoying it.

Claire: I have my art materials out and I am doing as you suggested. The yellow is creamy, thick and rich and stands up in a swirl. It makes me think of butter or flower petals all tightly wound together ready to open up.

Soul Self: Good. Now paint a wide band of it across the top of the canvas as if it were a yellow sky and draw it down the canvas, letting it talk to you about what a yellow sky knows about being beautiful.

Claire: It flows on nicely and I like to apply it good and thick. Now I'm thinking about a sky, which is ordinarily blue, being yellow instead. The yellow light is saying it will be a mellow day full of soft sun, maybe a bit overcast, but with light bouncing off of everything in diffuse shades of yellow. Wow, I never noticed that before about a sunrise. It foretells the day! I did hear what the yellow sky had to say, just by paying attention to it. Oh, now I understand what you meant by waiting and looking instead of just going on to something else. It all does unfold and it feels happy.

OK, I got that, but what do I do with the rest of the painting? I now have a completely yellow sky.

Soul Self: You can record the sunrise by leaving the yellow along the horizon and then blending the yellow into blue higher in the sky. Of course, some layers of sky will be a bit green as the two colors mix. They will look like clouds lit from the bottom in yellow but still be blue on the top. It will be beautiful.

Claire: That's a good idea. I'm working on it now. Yes, there's the green layer. Now I'm blending to pure blue. I think I'll put a bit of white in with the green to suggest clouds. Oh, this looks nice. But now what do I do in the foreground? All I have is sky.

Soul Self: Let's see if it could be a nice seaside scene. With a rich blue at the top of the painting, create some blue water in the foreground. Later, we'll add a beach and maybe some boats. Remember the golden yellow will be reflected on the blue water as highlights.

Claire: OK, I got that. Let's see how this works out. I want to use several shades of blue for the water and maybe a little green to show the many colors in water and the waves on the surface. Here goes.

Soul Self: Wow! That looks wonderful, doesn't it?

Claire: I'm glad that you like it. I love it, too. OK, now the joyful feeling is coming. I feel happy. It's working, just like you said. Such fun. By the way, do you see what I see with my eyes?

Soul Self: Yes, of course. We see and feel everything together. We are so alike at this moment, we are aware that we are a single being having two experiences merged together, much like the colors. This cooperation is what makes the feelings flow. You are feeling me as you and we are both feeling God, so we are all feeling love. It all works together. Are you wondering how we are going to do the beach? Guess what color?

Claire: Golden yellow for sand, of course. And then I'll add some dune grasses and maybe some boats tied up at a dock. I think that I am getting the ideas before you even tell me.

Soul Self: How could that be? Surely you jest! (Laughing)

Claire: (Laughing) You know what? We're both laughing and thinking the same thing at the same time.

Soul Self: Then why are we taking the time to write this down. We could just live our beautiful day together, letting our thoughts and happiness flow along and unfold on its own.

Claire: I don't know how we got to this point, but I think I know just what you mean. "Go with the flow, it's fun." (Laughing)

Claire put down her pen and her paintbrush and just sat in her chair with tears running down her face. They were tears of relief and joy and maybe the kind of tears Thelma has when her stories are so funny she just has to laugh and cry at the same time. Claire rested there in a kind of dreamy state of thought and perhaps she even fell asleep for a few moments. Nothing much mattered but the flow of the feeling of happiness.

Slowly, her energy began to rise and she felt the urge to get up and take a walk. It was such a beautiful day and she felt so good, walking would be wonderful. She took a long drink of water and descended the stairs, heading onto the sidewalk with a confident stride. She immediately noticed the spring wild flowers bouncing in the grass in Thelma's yard- grape hyacinths, crocus and tiny dandelions. The grass seemed to send the colorful flowers shooting up and the flowers bounced in the wind to say thank you. These small plants were part of their own small community of life just underfoot. Everything in it belonged there, cooperated with everything else and was quite beautiful.

Looking more closely, she noticed the fine details of the flower petals and leaves supported by the stems. She saw little insects drinking from the depths of the flowers and caught the scent that drew them. She suddenly knew why they came to the sweet and fragrant flowers. She felt the happiness of the little insect wings flapping and spinning very fast. All of this was only exceeded by the loud hum of a hummingbird diving into the feast of tulips by the mailbox. The hummingbird let out its long tongue and greedily sipped the nectar. *That's where it gets its energy*, Claire thought. *It lives moment by moment on the sweetness of its host flowers. Without the constant supply of nectar, it would not have the energy to fly.*

She had wanted to take a brisk walk, but was hardly past the mailbox, enthralled with what she had found already. Making her way down the street she made the acquaintance of the different trees, each having different bark and leaves. Some smelled sweet and others tart. Some trees were deeply rooted and could stand for centuries while others had more shallow roots, intending to rest in the neighborhood for only a decade or two. The blades of grass and branches of trees attested to the great adaptability of plant life; one was very small and frail and the other very large and sturdy. One kind of life in two very different forms, so much like she and Soul Self.

If she had been in a musical movie, she would have danced and sang. As it was, she was speechless and didn't walk very far at all. She saw just too much to appreciate and enjoy in the half block she had explored, so she decided wherever she was she wanted to be happy, being completely safe and free to do so. After about an hour, she returned to the porch to sit on the swing, thinking about the experience of joy just beyond the fear and self-doubt that had clouded her perception of reality. She felt the sun on her face and breeze on her arms and remained there until lunchtime called her to the kitchen for a salad and a drink.

Later, she returned to the art materials and painted another painting of the flowers and the insects as she had come to know them and their relationships with each other. By the time this painting was finished, she knew the flowers and insects as individual beings of grace and charm, working together to unfold life in ever more complex and refined ways. Then she looked at both the beach and the flower painting from a distance and found them satisfying as a subtle way of communicating what she had felt. Even though she had a lot to learn about painting techniques, she saw her homey depictions of familiar, commonplace reality in a beautiful way.

Wanting to see the paintings in the sunlight, she walked outside into the yard, where her neighbor Alfred leaned over the wood garden fence and he asked to see her artwork. Claire had so often seen the neighbor working in his rose garden for hours on end, perfectly content with no one else around. She knew he would understand.

Alfred looked at the paintings for a long time and said, " I see that you have found the work of the insects interesting. You can't have a garden without them, lots of them. Come into my garden and I'll show you my tulips."

They walked around the garden talking, about the flowers and insects and admiring the variety of colors, shapes and scents. Clearly, this kind of experience is addictive, Claire thought. No wonder Alfred continued to live there alone, tending his late wife's garden in contentment. She inquired about his life with Eileen.

Always happy to talk of his beloved wife, Alfred began. "When we first met, Eileen was tending flowers at a nursery and I was in a trades program to be a mechanic. One day I stopped and started talking to her as she worked. I offered to sharpen her tools for her because I knew immediately I wanted to be near her. I guess I loved her from the first moment she touched my hand. She was so gentle and quiet. I had come from a large family with lots of noise and conflict, but I always was the quiet one myself and she was just like me." Claire smiled and nodded, encouraging him to continue.

"Well, after high school, I signed up to serve in the Navy and became an airplane mechanic. When I got out, I had good benefits and had saved some money, so I asked her to marry me. She simply said yes and we got married in a rose garden much like this one. It took a lot of years of hard work, but we bought this house and raised four children. She worked in this garden whenever she could. We expected to grow old together and we did, but I didn't realize how hard it would be when she died first. She gave me her life and I never let her down, but she died first."

Alfred's voice cracked and tears welled up from deep inside of him, which he was helpless to control. Claire waited respectfully until he relaxed. Finally, she said, "You two were happy together and that is a great blessing. I suspect this garden still makes you happy."

"Yes," Alfred composed himself and added, "You can come over anytime and look at the flowers and maybe paint some paintings. I'd love that."

At that moment, the school bus stopped in front of the house. Alexa saw the two by the fence and came to talk. Claire explained that Alfred had invited them to paint the flowers in his garden. Alexa laughed and said that first she'd have to learn how to paint anything. They chatted for some minutes, said thanks and good bye to Alfred. The two then came into the house for an after school snack and Alexa talked about her day at school.

"I almost got into a fight today in band class. Justin was picking on Teddy again because he's small and slow to learn the songs. I don't know what Justin thinks gives him the right to bully anybody. I told him I'd punch his lights out if he didn't stop, but the teacher stepped in and took them to the principal's office."

"I think we'd better talk to Thelma about this," Claire said, recognizing a dangerous situation that had recently made the news in other schools. "Did the teacher say anything to you?"

"Just that I should have called his attention to the problem, and not threatened to punch Justin. I guess he was right," replied Alexa. "It just made me mad and I wasn't going to back down."

"Just like your grandmother, I suppose, but it's always better to get help from your teachers. So what else happened at school?" Claire guided the discussion to other topics.

"Well, school will be out in two weeks for summer vacation. I want to go to the swimming pool every day and sign up for summer camp at the recreation center. They have a drawing and painting class this summer," enthused Alexa.

"Sounds good to me," replied Claire, wondering how Thelma would want to schedule Alexa's comings and goings.

"Then my Mom will get out of prison," said Alexa, her voice tinged with apprehension.

"Yes, that'll come soon enough. We need to talk about that, don't we?" said Claire, intending to bring all of these concerns to the supper table this evening. "But for now, let's take some time to get your homework done and maybe enjoy this beautiful day."

At supper, Thelma responded briefly to the story about bullying. "You should know better than to threaten someone, but I am proud of you for standing up for what's right." Alexa nodded, knowing Thelma would have done the same as she and probably more.

Turning to the topic of Annabelle's release, Thelma announced she'd signed up Annabelle for a halfway house program for inmates with histories of drug addiction. Thelma planned to pick her up at the release center and drive directly to the place, where Annabelle would be subject to a curfew.

"Can she go out during the day?" asked Claire, wondering how much trouble Annabelle could get into during the day without supervision.

"Yes, but she has to be in by 8 p.m. or lose her privileges. Just to be safe, I applied for a court order, requiring her to stay away from this house unless invited. I want you, Claire, to be with Alexa every minute unless she's at Diana's house with Cassie or summer camp. Last year I paid Diana for summer childcare and it worked out pretty well. If Annabelle comes to the house, call the police immediately. I will explain all of this to her before she gets out." Thelma had outlined her plan, but she looked far from content.

"What do you think will happen to her?" asked Alexa.

"I don't know, but it won't be easy. Nothing ever is with her. The most important thing is she not bring trouble to us," Thelma said in a determined voice.

"We've been praying for her. Maybe it will go better than we think," hoped Claire. The others nodded and then changed the subject.

That night in her notebook, Claire asked her Soul Self what was going to happen with Annabelle and got a reassuring, but not very specific answer: "Better than expected and much more good than bad. All is well, do not be afraid." With that, Claire elected to put all worries aside and sat at her window recalling the joys of the day, the heartfelt story of Alfred and Eileen and the prospect of a fun summer with Alexa. She especially enjoyed watching the sunset, which was just as beautiful as the sunrise.

Ever so gently, the bright sun that had brought forth the beautiful day slithered out of sight and night quietly proceeded to fall. But the setting sun also left the promise that dawn would arise again in another beautiful sunrise as if, once again, time did not matter. For just as the sun rises the same on a day of peace as on a day of disaster, everything unfolds in a good way when it can be viewed without fear and the intention is right. To see it any other way is to be blind to oneself. Such was the test of fate Annabelle was about to discover.

Chapter 13:
A Turning Point

If indeed, intention is everything, which intention would it be that would determine the next events in Annabelle's life? Was it her intention to reconnect with her friends in the drug gang and resume her role as drug queen? Or was it the humble and hopeful intention of her family that she rebuild her life into a good one? Once an intention or set of intentions becomes active in the passage of events, even if in conflict, as these were, then much happens that is a mix of good and bad. In this case it was to come in rapid succession.

The long-dreaded day of Annabelle's release finally arrived and as she sat in the release center waiting for her mother to sign the papers and end her discussion with the authorities, Annabelle appeared determined, but silent. In the car Thelma began to advise her as to how to get along after release. Annabelle had anticipated this and, being used to appearing to be cooperative to get along in prison life, she said nothing. But deep in her heart, a fire that had been smoldering for ten years was enflamed to life. It was the fire to be what she had once been in the drug world and then some. She anticipated it would be easy as she was now much more aware of how cops operated. She was sure to get away with whatever she wanted.

Thinking about her old friends and the lovely feeling of being high, she was sure her life was finally getting better and she wanted it, no matter what the consequences were.

After Thelma dropped her daughter at the halfway house, Annabelle quickly saw life there was much like that in prison- the food was bland, the rooms minimal, and the company the same. But this place had the option of some freedom between the hours of 8 a.m. and 8 p.m. Shortly after arriving, she walked out on her own and headed down the street to her old favorite drug hang-outs with fun on her mind.

One such place was Pat's Bar. Finding nobody she knew, she positioned herself beside a nice-looking young man whose eyes widened when she pressed against his leg. One drink followed another and soon they were in bed in a small motel room, getting high and having sex. Her spirits soared. She was still the queen. She was happy.

As day turned into night, the young man rose to leave, but Annabelle stayed the night, missing her curfew. In the morning, she searched bars and alleys for a connection. Without any money, she was rushed on her way. Finally, she met the current gang leader and challenged him for her rightful place in the gang.

"I taught you all you know. Now move over, I'm back and taking over."

"You loser, don't you see what a narc-magnet you are? Get out of here and don't come back."

"I'll stay as long as I want. Go f___k yourself, you're just a baby."

The gang leader raised his hand to summon a thug, who took Annabelle by her arms and dragged her outside to the ally.

There she screamed, fought and kicked while he beat her on the neck and head. At last she dropped unconscious where he left her bleeding and badly injured. It wasn't long before the police found her.

Thelma was at work when she got the call from the police. The officer described what had happened to Annabelle and where she was hospitalized. It was with a heavy heart that Thelma immediately drove to the emergency room and saw Annabelle unconscious with cuts and bruises, two broken ribs and a dislocated right shoulder. Worst of all, one blow to her head had caused intracranial bleeding and swelling, possibly damaging the retina. It was likely Annabelle could suffer some loss of brain function and maybe diminished sight in her right eye, but the doctors thought she would regain consciousness. Meanwhile she was on pain medications and slept. As day turned into night, Thelma left to go home and thought about her daughter as the beautiful baby girl with dark red hair she had loved and raised. Now she saw a disabled woman in her thirties unable to control her own behavior. While Thelma loved her, she hated the harm Annabelle seemed to bring to them both.

Being a realist, Thelma rarely gave way to sentimentality, but on this dark night, she cried for her child and the potential that she would be a cripple or lose the sight of one eye for life. It was so sad and so unnecessary. Where would Annabelle go? Who would take care of her? The answer to the last question resided in Thelma's tears. Despite her earlier refusal to take her in, Thelma now resolved, if possible, she would take care of Annabelle at home. Her logic was she wasn't likely to get into trouble in her condition, and the drug gang had rejected her. Moreover, no one but her family would love and care for her. But how could Thelma and her little family cope with this turn of events? Upon arriving home, she began to discuss the problem with Alexa and Claire.

"Well, Annabelle's done it now! She's been beaten and is in the hospital unconscious. She has broken ribs, a dislocated shoulder and swelling in her brain," announced Thelma at the supper table with Alexa and Claire following the story with many questions in mind.

"Do they think she'll recover?" asked Alexa.

"Yes, but they don't know how disabled she'll be. I think it all depends on how strong she is and what care she gets. A lot of good luck would help," replied Thelma.

"I'm willing to try to help her if she can be cared for at home," proposed Claire.

"Me, too," joined Alexa, adding Thelma's typical comment, "But it won't be easy."

"You got that right," muttered Thelma. "God help us."

"Ditto," all thought with sincerity.

Thelma spent the next few days visiting therapists, doctors and nursing facilities trying to ascertain what therapies Annabelle would need and what services they could get for free or at a low cost. In the end, the long road to recovery was outlined in a detailed schedule, consisting of appointment after appointment with doctors and therapists. There was always the risk Annabelle could have repeated strokes and setbacks, making the outcome uncertain, but the process was clear. Within a few days, Annabelle was conscious and later was released to Thelma's care. At the hospital discharge desk, Annabelle sat in a wheelchair, able to see with one eye and having only minimal and slurred speech. She was helped into Thelma's car and they headed for the duplex in silence.

Upon arrival at home, Thelma pulled up close to the back door and got the wheelchair out of the trunk. Claire and Alexa, who had been waiting to see what lay ahead for them, quickly ran to help carry the wheelchair into the house. Ever so slowly and gently, Claire and Thelma helped Annabelle out of the car, up the stairs and finally back into the wheelchair. After wheeling her into the living room, they all stood around appraising the situation while Annabelle vacantly looked at the floor. Finally, Thelma put her hands on her hips and announced, "Well, ladies, this is going to have to be a homemade miracle! And Annabelle you're going to cooperate or you'll sit in this chair the rest of your life. You were better off in prison."

They could not have known it, but Thelma's prediction reached Annabelle's heart where she heard her future being determined by Thelma and it made her mad. Meanwhile, Alexa and Claire began to ask questions.

"Where will she sleep, Thelma?" queried Alexa.

"For now, she'll sleep in my bedroom so if she needs help in the middle of the night, I'll hear her. We'll bring in Claire's spare single bed from the garage."

Alexa needed to know more. " What do we do to help her?"

"I have a list of doctors and therapists she has to see on a regular basis. We'll find out what they say."

Then Claire joined in. "Can she go to the bathroom by herself?"

"If we get her a walker, she might be able to, but for now, to keep her from falling, we'll have to hold her arms."

"Can she talk?" asked Alexa.

"I think a little, but she won't. She's mad at the world and us in particular, so don't expect much gratitude."

Thoughtfully, Alexa commented. "She needs some comfortable clothes. She can't wear the hospital gown all of the time."

"We can lend her a nightgown and some sweats for now," Thelma suggested

"I have some that should fit her and I can do them with my laundry. Later we can go to Charity Thrift and get her some pretty things. When is her first doctor's appointment?" Claire was seeing a way to make a plan.

"In two weeks. Here are the discharge papers with some instructions to follow. Enough questions! I'm going to fix some soup and sandwiches for lunch . . . after I have a cigarette." It was the first cigarette that Thelma had smoked in a long time.

With that, Annabelle raised her head and gestured she would like a cigarette as well, which raised the possibility in Thelma's mind that Annabelle could be motivated to cooperate by using rewards. Thelma rolled Annabelle out to the front porch, but did not give her a cigarette. There they sat in silence, Thelma thinking about using rewards to get Annabelle to cooperate, while Annabelle struggled to voice her opinion of Thelma. The word came out "beach."

"Keep trying, you'll get it right," Thelma replied.

Meanwhile, Alexa and Claire poured over the hospital instructions and made a list of the doctor appointment times. Going to her computer, Alexa began to research therapies under the topics of head injuries and stroke. She and Claire read and discussed what they found until Thelma called them for lunch during which they discussed what the articles had to say about head injuries. Surprisingly, Annabelle was hungry and eagerly ate what was offered to her. That made Claire think about dietary approaches to enhance recovery and asked Alexa to research that as well. After lunch they brought the bed from the garage into the house, cleaned it up and set it up to be Annabelle's place of rest in Thelma's room.

The makings of the homemade miracle were beginning to form with fresh clean sheets and a flowered nightgown laid out on the end of the bed. The bed was placed close to the bathroom so Annabelle did not have far to go. Surprisingly, Annabelle laid down on the bed and quickly fell asleep. Seeing an opportunity to do some shopping, Claire and Alexa went to the discount store and bought a toothbrush, hairbrush, some makeup, hair ties, hand lotion and women's sanitary pads Annabelle would need to be comfortable. When they returned, they put the things on a table by Annabelle's bed, not surprised to see that Thelma had also gone to sleep in her bed. They returned to their Internet research, focusing on dietary recommendations. By suppertime, they had worked out a schedule of appointments and therapeutic exercises from the discharge instructions and posted the schedule on the refrigerator. Under it, they posted a list of suggestions for the care and feeding of such patients. If each of the three agreed to sign up for one or two items on the list each day, together, they thought, they could keep up with Annabelle's needs.

Proud of what they had accomplished, Claire and Alexa worked in the kitchen to prepare a good supper for the four. As they worked on the meal, they talked about Thelma and what help she would need, praying that the homemade miracle would work. But in the end it wasn't that any of the four knew exactly what to do or how to do it. They only knew they had to try. Thus a new pattern of life began for them, one that held no harm and lots of willingness for good.

Both Thelma and Annabelle were roused for the evening meal and all seated around the table, Annabelle sitting in the wheelchair at one end and Thelma at the other. Everyone ate the meal of bean soup, ham sandwiches and salad in a virtual silence, very uncharacteristic of the family. After supper, they all sat on the porch to enjoy the evening, while thinking about the events of the day and plans to come. Much to everyone's comfort and support, while their human minds were thinking about the problems ahead, their Soul Selves were giving help and assistance.

Thelma's Human Mind: I know that I'm not the cause of all of this, but this is a serious complication in my life. I feel like I've had enough of this. How am I going to pay for all of this?

Thelma's Soul Self: Consider having Annabelle declared an indigent disabled person, so she'll qualify for free health services and food stamps. You can take the hospital discharge papers to the social services office and they will help you.

Alexa's Human Mind: She's my Mom, but is physically just like a baby, only with a mean and hard heart. No wonder Thelma took me away from her when I was little. Annabelle would have ruined my life as well as her own. Thank you, Thelma.

Alexa's Soul Self: You are now a great resource for Annabelle. Because of the love and support Thelma gives you, you'll be able to help Annabelle recover. Provide her with DVD's and TV shows on useful and positive topics she's never thought about.

Claire's Human Mind: Her arms seem so limp and she can't walk or stand very well. I wonder if there's anything I can do to help her regain her balance and strength.

Claire's Soul Self: Massage her skin with lotion, especially the joints. The circulation and movement of the ligaments and muscles will stimulate the nerves to regain their function. It will go better than you expect. I'll help you every step of the way.

Annabelle's Human Mind: Crap! How did I get to be this way? Now I don't have a life at all. They don't want me in the gang and I don't want to live here with these do-gooders. I'd do anything for a cigarette and a beer right now.

Annabelle's Soul Self: I know you're not listening to me, but the others are trying to help you for your own good, proof you are loved and therefore good. You'll soon find you can do good when you put your mind to it. You are a Beloved One and you'll recover only as fast as you become convinced of that. For now, you are safe and being cared for. It's best you cooperate.

The day having been a tiring one and the days to come promising to be much the same, they all decided to go to bed early. They did so with the confidence they had in each other and the little thoughts of help their Soul Selves had offered. From such little seeds of kindness and with such rich resources of mind and heart, there was hope they would succeed. Just to reassure each they were all present and engaged in the mutual effort, they said goodnight to each other while leaving the porch.

"Goodnight, Claire and Alexa," called Thelma.

"Goodnight, Thelma," replied Claire.

"Goodnight, Thelma," replied Alexa.

"Goodnight, Annabelle," finished Thelma. There was no response, and Annabelle was not the least bit grateful for the gift of a homemade miracle on her behalf. However, she would never again so quickly reject the offers of help, partly because she had few other options, but also because the prospect of being confined to a wheelchair for the rest of her life was more abhorrent than living with the three. Her decision to choose something better for herself would prove to be the most important part of the family's homemade miracle.

Chapter 14:
Where There's a Schedule, There's a Way

For the weeks to come, life was ruled by the schedule of doctor's appointments, patient care instructions and list of suggestions for head injury patients posted on the refrigerator door. Each day everyone signed up for something, until all of the duties were checked and completed. As Claire and Alexa tried some of the suggestions, they found some worked for their patient and some did not and so each week, the list was updated and changed for the better.

Other people in the neighborhood were also offering help. Typically Thelma paid Diana to watch Alexa during the summer, so she decided to ask Diana to watch both Alexa and Annabelle four days a week in Thelma's house until Claire got home from work. Diana needed the money and had some patient care experience, so the deal was formed and she proved to be a reliable and wise caregiver.

Alfred, who lived next door, noticed Annabelle was using a wheelchair and he volunteered to make a wood ramp to fit over the stairs to accommodate the wheelchair. Once he had installed the ramp, he also invited Annabelle to sit in his rose garden if she wanted to get out of the house.

The first week, Thelma had taken another day off from work to visit the county social services offices where she applied for Annabelle to be accepted as an indigent disabled person. This entitled her to free health services, medications, a walker and shower stool, food stamps and even to apply for a monthly income check through Social Security. Thelma was delighted and vowed to never again complain about paying taxes, as all of these services were at taxpayer expense. If the disability benefit was approved, she planned to use the monthly disability income to buy Annabelle some clothes and food and to pay Diana for the daycare. At some point, Thelma hoped to open a savings account for Annabelle so she could someday get her own place. It would take the services of an attorney to win the benefit, but it would be worth it. However, the free healthcare and food stamps were enough to provide Annabelle with nutritious meals and basic care. All in all, Thelma realized being able to pay for her daughter's care was not the problem she had initially thought.

With the end of the school year imminent, Alexa was studying for finals, but had some time to order some DVD's from the library for Annabelle to develop an interest in a more positive world. She also checked the program schedule for the local Public Television Channel and searched on her movie rental account for topics such as history, cooking, travel, science, documentaries, arts and crafts. With plenty to be found, Alexa only had to write the schedule of the programs on the list and the others made sure Annabelle would be watching. Actually, Alexa loved these topics herself, and after exams, the two would often watch the programs together. As the weeks progressed, Annabelle began to take an interest and new bonds of awareness were being formed between mother and daughter as they viewed the programs together. After several weeks of the program viewing, Alexa brought some of the topics to the supper table.

"Thelma, guess what year the civil war ended?" Alexa posed a quiz at the supper. Thelma said that she knew, but couldn't remember, but Annabelle slurred the words "Eightsheen seeshy shive. Thelma was impressed and said, "Ask another question."

"When did Prohibition end?" Annabelle mumbled something that couldn't be understood, but Alexa smiled and gave her a high-five gesture. This time, Claire asked for another question.

"Who was the last queen of Egypt?" Alexa asked. Annabelle paused for a moment and then pointed to herself. They waited to understand what she could possibly be saying and slowly realized she'd made a joke. They all laughed, amazed at her audacity.

+

Claire continued her counseling sessions. At Claire's second session, Scott followed the same procedure as before, welcoming her and taking notes. He continued asking questions about Claire's life and family.

"Did you ever have any major health issues, accidents or other crises in your life?"

"No, I've been pretty healthy and had a fairly normal life, I guess."

"Do you use drugs or alcohol to excess?"

"Of course not. Mom and Dad were very strict with us and we were religious. I wasn't even allowed to date anyone who drank. Actually, I didn't date much until my twenties," Claire declared, suddenly wondering about how strict her life had been.

"Did you feel depressed as a child?"

"Well, yes, I did. I never had much confidence in myself. I always wondered if I was doing things right."

"You mentioned that religion was a strong factor in your family. Tell me about your religious education. What was it like to be you in your church? Were there aspects of your religious upbringing that caused you concern?" Scott was beginning to see a possible source of a problem.

"I loved to go to church and pray. I would even go to church during the week when nobody else was there and sit and look at the stained glass windows and statues. It made me feel good. But now I think of it, I was always told to sacrifice myself for others. So I tried to always put others first. My brother Ernie never believed in self-sacrifice. He said everybody has to take care of themselves." Claire paused while memories played in her mind.

"Do you still pray?"

"Yes, I pray for everyone. I prayed for my husband, but it didn't help. He died anyway." Suddenly, Claire felt angry. "I sacrificed everything for him and he died."

"I can see this upsets you," paused Scott. "Let's take a minute to think about this. Your religion taught you to put others first and yourself second, which you did in the case of your husband. You expected for it to turn out better and it didn't. Is that what you are thinking?"

"Well, yeah!" Claire responded hotly and then retreated. "I'm sorry, I don't have any right to be angry."

"I think that your brother Ernie is right, Claire. You have the right and responsibility to take care of yourself and to have equality in your relationships. Maybe you misunderstood your religious teachings." Scott knew he had touched a real problem in Claire's life. "I see how this belief would have caused you to lack confidence in yourself. And by the way, you have every right to express your emotions in a responsible way."

Claire was stunned at the simple statement Scott had made. Had she really thought that she didn't have the right to take care of herself? Had she indeed misunderstood her religion? She didn't know what to say. There was a long silence and then,

"Are you saying what I was taught was wrong?"

"It's not anyone's fault, it's just a misunderstanding from your childhood and you can make it right anytime you want," Scott continued.

"Why would I believe it so long and Ernie didn't?"

"I don't know, but many women of your generation thought the same thing for a long time. Many of them realized the error and became more independent. I'm not asking you to change your religious beliefs, only to be reasonable about them."

"I must have missed that."

"How was your relationship with your husband?"

"He was the one with a good job in the family and I took care of the home and worked part-time."

"Perhaps your upbringing, religion and economic situation conspired to keep you in submissive thinking for a long time," Scott proposed. "It's not your fault."

"So what do I do now?" asked Claire, unsure of herself once again.

"Well, I think we'll talk about ways in which you can be equal in your relationships and put your own needs first in your decision-making, then help others after that. I wonder if this is why you sometimes felt depressed. What do you think?"

"Looks like it, doesn't it," sighed Claire. "I've been such a fool."

"Not a fool, just a person trying to do the right thing. You just need to be reasonable about things," proposed Scott again.

"Yeah, OK. I feel tired, can I go now?"

"Yes, you get to decide that, Claire. If you feel tired, then we will stop for now and continue the next time," assured Scott. "See you in one week, same time, same place. Please know I think you are a fine person. You are not a failure at anything I can see."

"Thanks." Claire left before she started to cry once again. Scott had given her a lot to consider and it was essentially the same thing that Thelma and Ernie had been telling her for a long time.

+

The days Claire was at home, she was responsible for Alexa, but also for Annabelle's meals, bathroom needs, driving to appointments and general housekeeping for an invalid. Each day she massaged Annabelle's skin and joints with lotion. The other days, Diana took the same duties until Claire came home from work. On the weekends everyone took turns. With Annabelle needing so much sleep to recover, they found life could go on without unfairly burdening any one member of the family.

However, the miracle held a significant surprise on the day of Annabelle's first doctor's appointment. Preparing Annabelle for her appointment, Claire gave her a shower and shampooed her hair. Thelma had laid out a nice shirt and stretch pants for her to wear, having bought her lots of nice new underwear. It was a day for Annabelle to get out of the house and Claire wanted to make it a happy cheerful time.

The clinic they attended was housed in a new building funded by recently provided federal grants to improve infrastructure for emergency and health services. It was a beautiful, big building, but the waiting room still could not accommodate all of the people needing help. The wait to see a doctor was determined by the number of people waiting, the sequence of signing in and the reason for the visit, so they sat for some time waiting. At last, the nurse called Annabelle's name to come to an exam room and Claire remained in the waiting room. The nurse took Annabelle's weight and height, blood pressure and pulse, asking for a urine sample for a pregnancy test as a standard policy. She then completed notes in the medical chart. That left Annabelle alone in the exam room, waiting for the doctor.

When the doctor arrived, he began by reading the nurses' notes, and presently congratulated Annabelle on being pregnant. Noticing that Annabelle held her breath, he cautiously asked if she wanted to talk about the pregnancy. Annabelle said nothing, so the doctor recommended prenatal vitamins and gave a referral to an ob/gyn doctor down the hall. Continuing on with the neural exam, he checked Annabelle's nerve responses and the sight in her eyes. He noted that progress was moderately good and said she could start physical therapy next week. He wrote the PT orders on the chart, which alerted the nurse to give Annabelle an envelope full of instructions. The nurse showed her out and she and Claire went to the window to pay the deductible and to schedule the next appointment. Seeing the thick envelope of instructions, Claire knew it contained more information for the refrigerator schedule. The next checkup would be in another two weeks, then monthly after that.

All of this time, Annabelle said little and was deep in thought about being pregnant. She had been pregnant before, but this time was different for her. Although she had been given little choice in Alexa's rearing, this time she wanted to keep the baby. She was in her thirties and the drug gang lifestyle was no longer an option for her, so the baby was all she had in the world. How she was going to raise it was a complete unknown to her, for she knew little about babies or childcare, but she would manage- or could she? She looked at herself in the wheelchair in the window and saw she was an invalid. She wasn't even sure if she was strong enough to deliver the child.

In the car on the way home, Claire did not say much to Annabelle, sensing her need to think. However, when they arrived home, Thelma was eager to hear the report from the doctor and quickly scanned the doctor's notes and instructions. When she got to the part about the pregnancy, Thelma's face got red and her whole body shook. She looked at Annabelle and locked her mouth tight in rage. Turning, she stalked to her room and slammed the door. There she slammed more doors and kicked shoes around. As drawers were going in and out, there were a few "Oh, my God!" exclamations. In fact, Thelma had pulled out her suitcase from the closet and was packing it. She reasoned the time had come to just walk away from this person who was destroying her life and that of others. Thinking about it for a moment longer, she then unpacked the bag, returning it to the closet and reentered the living room. She spun Annabelle around to face her and said in a low but determined voice, nose to nose, "You will get better and raise this child. And you are going to do a good job of it, because I am not going to. You are not going to ruin this baby's life like you have done mine. Do you hear me? Am I clear?"

For once, Annabelle nodded her head yes and sucked in a deep breath. Thelma went out for a cigarette, and Claire and Alexa went to the kitchen in silent amazement at what had just happened. Annabelle sat alone in the living room and raised her head, looking up at the ceiling. She thought to herself: "God help me." Then tears flowed and she heaved and heaved, gulping in grief for over an hour. No one interrupted her, as they knew something had finally moved her heart. In one surprising day, she was faced with the choice of changing from a rebellious addict bent on self-destruction to someone who cared about someone else. However, having someone to love, she also had someone to lose. She had someone who would love her, but for whom she would have to give care and support. She had never felt this way before, ever.

The prospect of having a baby should be a happy and wonderful experience for anyone, but to Thelma it was outrageously irresponsible. To Annabelle, it was both infuriating and terrifying to have her life so constrained in a direction she did not want it to go, but yet, she felt the power of it. To Claire it demanded respect and joyful anticipation of caring for a child, which she never had for herself. To Alexa it meant the wonderment of a sibling. But certainly, they all knew this challenge would require Annabelle to heal her damaged nervous system, learn about pregnancy and raising children, change her lifelong attitudes of rebellion and stubbornness, overcome addiction and acquire life skills such as discipline, patience, wisdom and perseverance. There was a huge gap, make that a gargantuan gap, between what Annabelle was now and what she needed to be for the sake of the baby.

It would be only by sheer determination and a whole lot of help that Annabelle could raise this child successfully. No amount of doubt could be admitted to the mix or the whole thing would collapse. But buried deep in her DNA and living under the veil of addiction and arrogance, Annabelle was just as determined as Thelma. This basic resource of determination shared by mother and child, set in place a long time ago, was the best hope for the future of this new child.

Not wanting to speak to each other or even to eat, everyone retired to their rooms and let the day creep to its only possible ending, rest. In the privacy of her room, Claire opened her notebook and began to converse with her Soul Self.

Claire: I think I know why Annabelle had all of this happen to her. Was it because she needed to be helpless, but also to care for someone else who was helpless?

Soul Self: Yes, indeed. This is a turning event in which she can experience being loved as well as giving love. Did we ever talk about the life path of a human being in the physical plane? It would be a good way to understand what's happening in this little home.

Claire: Well, Thelma's explanation is that before incarnation, souls make agreements with each other to be in the lifetime together and to do certain things. But that's all I know. Could you tell me more?

Soul Self: Before incarnation, a soul makes a plan for the coming lifetime of the human mind. When one selects a lifetime of resistance to love or consciously intends harm due to fear, that person has to operate under the law of karma. If a person accepts being loved and cooperates with the guidance of the soul for good, then the lifetime is organized under the law of grace. Karma provides defining turning events so the person has to choose to turn from fear to love. Essentially, negative intentions yield negative consequences bringing one to the conclusion that intending good is much better. The law of Grace consists of intending good, which unfolds into more good.

When two souls enter into the earth plane for the purpose of living their lives together, whether coming together for a moment or for the whole lifetime, their cooperation together is designed to forward both upon their own path, perhaps one karmic and the other graceful. To have them living together is a great gift of love, for each has their own intentions and life plans, one the hard way and the other the easy way. However, both end with the same ultimate conclusion: Love is the only way to go.

In the case of Thelma and Annabelle, Thelma wants a happy family life, which consists of grace unfolding into more grace. Annabelle wants to be the one who hates what Thelma wants and destroys as much of it as possible. It is a classic Karma/Grace interaction. Because love is all there is, Annabelle will experience such consequences until she turns in the direction of love. Each is coming from a different point, but both moving to the same conclusion.

Therefore, what you witnessed today was Thelma announcing Annabelle's turning point has arrived. She demanded Annabelle turn from a harmful intention to a good one and as it was their pre-incarnation agreement to have this confrontation, it cannot be avoided. Annabelle asked for help and her Soul moved to empower the human Annabelle to turn toward grace. The changes will begin to unfold as the days and weeks go by. Certainly, there will be setbacks, but each time these two confront each other in honesty, they will have to make the same decision to love this child over and over again until the choice stands firmly without doubt.

Moreover, there is a third party to this agreement, the unborn child. This soul will be born in a body to be a strong translator between the higher plane and the human. Thus, the child's actions will always challenge Thelma and Annabelle to choose over and over again to cooperate with grace and to leave grief behind. This is a grand soul, in full agreement with the lifetime ahead.

You and Alexa will also have a role to play because you agreed to be together for this event. Thus, Alexa will teach Annabelle how to research what she needs to learn. You will teach Annabelle patience and discipline as well as to see beauty. All members of this human and spiritual family will be making contributions to their own benefit as well as for each other. I know this is a lot to understand, but it is essentially what all lifetimes are about, only different in the particulars, intentions and paths.

Claire: I think it is wonderful to have this explained so clearly. I plan to keep writing in my notebook, so I don't forget.

Soul Self: Such is your life plan. Even if only one person reads your notes and uses conscious cooperation with their own Soul Self to do great things, such as providing for their families, healing their bodies or doing beautiful things, they will be given great help to do so. Others may do things such as purifying polluted water, conserving energy, protecting endangered species, dealing with global warming, curing illnesses and reducing poverty.

Claire: Well, I guess anyone could, it's their own Soul. I guess they could ask questions and get help such as I have done. Since the Great Oneness knows all of the information we need to live well, they could certainly give the help this planet needs. I was grateful for the bread recipe and the help to do paintings, but I never thought about questions so much more significant, like global warming. So how would a question like that go?

Soul Self: If someone had educated him or herself in the sciences and had the determination to find a viable answer, then it only takes learning how to listen for the wisdom of the Soul to advance his or her knowledge. Then he or she would gather fellow scientists to work together and design experiments to verify the new information given through higher intelligence. Once that is accomplished, the group simply works from the first step to the last until they succeed. You can see there's an orderly process for doing such things.

Claire: A process for doing such things? Are you implying that a process has been available all along and maybe has even been used before?

Soul Self: That's where Alexa's interest in archeology comes in. When she's competent in the known information about archeology and uses conscious cooperation with her Soul Self, she can ask the Great Oneness questions for the benefit of society. Indeed it will start with explanations of how ancient societies used this process.

Claire: Really??? Give me an example of an ancient society that used this process.

Soul Self: The oldest known and best-documented civilization, which left great monuments to testify to its achievements, is that of the ancient Egyptians. They knew math, geometry, astronomy and the building trades from information given to them from the Great Oneness. In fact, they taught such skills to the Greeks and the Romans who also used them, recording these skills in their own languages, stories and myths.

Claire: Holy moly! You mean to say, what I am doing now with you, is the same as what the ancient Egyptians did, only they had better questions?

Soul Self: Yes, of course. You lived in those days, you know, and did a very good job of teaching just about anybody who asked how to ask the right questions and obtain valuable information. You were one of the great ones establishing the ground rules for doing so. This is about your fourth best lifetime.

Claire: Hold the phone a minute! I had past lives? Ground rules? Do I know all of this? Just how many lifetimes have I had? How come I don't remember them?

Soul Self: After you asked me to hold the phone, you asked three questions. Which question do you want me to answer first? This is a friendly and helpful conversation, after all, so we use a polite and organized way of having these discussions. By the way, courtesy is one of the ground rules; cooperation has to be friendly, personal, helpful and even humorous at all times. After all, we are in this together and if you succeed, we succeed.

Claire: I feel sort of lost here, but keep going on about the ground rules, please. If I could remember the ground rules, then I could be assured of constant and reliable contact. Is that what you are saying?

Soul Self: Yes, that is what you always said. The intention must always be for the Highest and Greatest Good; therefore no harm or even stress must come to anyone. After that, it is only required that you remain peaceful and have good questions. As such, you would be anticipating having a love affair with your Higher Self.

Your second question relates to having had a past life. Most humans have had many lives and display in their attributes, skills and abilities the results of the many experiences they have accumulated from these past lives. Using your human mind, you have difficulty remembering all of this, but using my mind, it is easy. Indeed, it might be a big step to try to remember the past lives, but it can be done. In fact, the third question implies that you could remember them if only you knew how. Just ask me to describe them to you is how.

Claire: This is amazing. I had no idea. So I get to use your mind? Now wait a minute, the book says that both are my minds, so I guess I could use either mind to do something good. OK, so let's assume I wanted to know about a past life. Help me to remember the lifetime when I knew the ground rules for making contact with you.

Soul Self: That would be an Egyptian life in the very ancient past. But since we are now in contact, it's obvious you know the ground rules; you just didn't realize it.

Take a recent experience as a great example of your knowledge of the ground rules. Do you remember when you were thoroughly enjoying making your bread, but wanted to make it better? First, you were at peace and second, you loved the experience of making bread. Third, you asked for help with a goal that constituted the Highest Good for you and everyone else. Lastly, you greatly appreciated it and wanted to learn more about where you got the information. It all led us to this conversation. Now do you see?

Claire: Yes, I see, but it all seemed so natural and easy. I didn't realize it would lead to this. Now that makes me think about what questions I could ask. To tell you the truth, I'd like to ask questions about solving pollution and global warming, but first I need to ask about the everyday things that make me happy. You feel like a best friend to me, like Thelma, and I love having our conversations and your wise help.

Soul Self: Would you like to ask about your forthcoming relationship with Mike?

Claire: What? I don't want a relationship with a man. I've had enough stress for this lifetime. OK, I admit I am curious to know if it would be possible for me to have a good relationship, no, it would have to be a great relationship. I feel like a schoolgirl worrying about boyfriends, but it is important to me. It would be to anyone.

Soul Self: Because we exist together in peaceful mutual support and help, we have to address this issue together. If you are not happy, I am not happy. That's the way it is.

Claire: OK, so go ahead and tell me about Mike. I'd love to hear what you have to say.

Soul Self: He's a man made of honesty, sincerely intending to help others, but he has come on hard times, much like you. Why don't you keep talking to him and see if you can help each other? That would be what friends do, as you said.

Claire: I suppose I could do that. Would you help me to not be afraid?

Soul Self: Of course. The first step is to just observe and talk to him as he comes and goes. You will learn a lot about being friends with him without feeling challenged.

Claire: OK, that's a deal.

Soul Self: Good, you have just canceled many appointments with disappointment. Your decision makes both of us happy. Now, your mind has been bent into a pretzel by our conversation, so why don't we give you a rest? We can continue tomorrow. Off to bed for now and sweet dreams.

Claire: We have opened the secret doorway of the universe between two worlds and know how to keep the doors open! How come there are no fireworks or bands playing to announce such good news? Everyone should know this. I feel so happy and light and free! What a grand feeling. Thank you for what you have told me tonight and thanks in advance for the great things that will come in future conversations. Good night.

Going to her bathroom to brush her teeth, she looked into the mirror and was shocked to find she looked confident, happy and excited. Indeed she had been told she was now a door opener to the Great Oneness, just as she had been long before. She was no longer the lonely widow burdened with grief, debt and misunderstanding. With that, she flicked the lights off and crawled into bed, not daring to even think anymore about what she had learned for fear she would never sleep again. But sleep did come rapidly, for in the ghostly light of night, much within her was to be repaired and upgraded by her Soul Self. Because her identity as an opener of the doorway between the physical and spiritual world had been recalled from a former life, she needed her body, mind, emotions and knowledge to be refitted to use those ancient skills and abilities to address the new tasks ahead of her.

If the night had been a movie, a huge white light would have shone over the humble duplex and the doors and windows would rumble, while weird music played. But as it was the real presence of a soul peacefully at work and not a Hollywood idea of extra terrestrials, the only thing happening was the gentle and peaceful rest of those who had reached turning points in their lives.

The curtains in Claire's window fluttered, blown by the early summer breeze like flags of inter-dimensional friendship. In Alexa's room, the same wind whispered memories of ancient peoples, and in Thelma's and Annabelle's room, the winds carried off mists of regret and painful memories, bringing deep rest. All was a sign the family of five were being silently but expertly refitted to move forward toward better lives for themselves and others.

Chapter 15:
Amazing Grace

As if nothing astounding had happened the day before, the next day began and ended with rain. It rained a cool, calming drizzle all day with only a few interruptions, temporarily washing away the dust and heat of the developing summer. It was very refreshing.

That day, Diana came to stay with Annabelle while Claire and Thelma worked. She also brought her dog, Shadow. Immediately as Diana and Shadow entered the living room, Shadow went to sniff Annabelle's feet and put his muzzle on her lap, looking up at her with beautiful brown dog eyes. Annabelle did not know how to react, so Diana asked Shadow to lie down and the dog obediently lay down beside Annabelle's wheelchair. There he looked at Diana with wise and patient eyes as if he, too, had volunteered to help with the homemade miracle.

Thelma had left instructions that Annabelle was to make her own bed, get dressed, and brush her teeth and hair on her own. Diana saw the wisdom of Thelma's requirements, but did assist Annabelle on a few aspects. As for Annabelle, she initially thought she wanted no part of being cared for by anyone, certainly not her family and their friend, but she was physically helpless to resist. Except for brushing her hair, the rather simple list proved quite a task for Diana and Annabelle to accomplish and the patient was exhausted by 10:00 a.m. Helping Annabelle to the couch, Diana massaged Annabelle's arms and legs with lotion and covered her with a light blanket. Annabelle quickly fell fast asleep.

Meanwhile, Claire had headed off to the bakery with many thoughts about Annabelle as well as the information from her notebook. Claire could think of thousands of questions regarding these events, but her day beckoned her into more mundane thoughts. At work, things were normal and she once again chatted with Ed as they began their day's work.

"Did I ever tell you I have Native American blood in me?" Ed ventured as a result of his recent thoughts about his Mother.

"No," replied Claire. " Tell me about it."

"Well, my Mother and Father were Cherokee and I was born on a reservation, but I remember little of it. When I was four, my mother and I moved to the city closest to the reservation and she got a job as a waitress. That didn't last very long as Natives weren't treated very well there, so we moved from job to job until we came to Cincinnati. By that time, I was able to help her out more at home, so we stayed here and I went to school. When I was old enough, I signed up with the army and served in Vietnam. When I came home, my Mother was in poor health and has since passed away," reminisced Ed. "She taught me so much of what's real in life, like the sunlight, the stars and the plants and animals of nature."

"What do you mean?" asked Claire, interested because of her experiences of stillness seeing plants as beautiful living consciousness.

"Well, it's not like my Mother taught me all of the old ceremonies or let me know a lot of the other members of my tribe, but I think I learned to see things differently than white people do." Ed searched for a way to describe what he meant and finally said, "I see the earth and all of it's life as my family. People are a part of it all, but not the most important part. I know that doesn't make much sense, but I have a distinct feeling I belong here along with all other life and we have to get along together. Actually, plants and animals are a lot easier to get along with than people."

"I've noticed that. I had a wonderful experience recently in which I could feel and appreciate so many forms of life, like the grass, insects and trees. It was a beautiful moment." Claire replied, sighing. "Are you saying all life has heart and soul, maybe even mind?"

"Yeah, that's it. It's sort of like, we're all here together, alive and sharing what's here to use," said Ed, stopping what he was doing to choose good words. "Yeah, that's it."

"That's a very wise way to see the world," said Claire. "It doesn't feel so alone to be alive in a world like that. Do you believe there are spirit beings here with us?"

"Native legends say so, so I guess so," replied Ed. "Why?"

"I've recently begun to think we are essentially spirit beings living in the earth and the spirit side of us is very wise and kind," offered Claire, not sure of how he would respond.

"If so, I hope the spirit side is a lot smarter than we are. People can be cruel and stupid," mused Ed. He did not dismiss Claire's proposed thought, as it did not conflict with anything he believed. In fact, the thought exceeded what he believed in a good and reasonable way, so he thought about it often.

"Did I tell you Annabelle's pregnant?" said Claire, changing the subject. "She's not yet able to walk by herself or talk very well, but she's pregnant. She's going to have to get a lot better before this child comes. Thelma got really mad when she found out about the baby. Good thing Annabelle can't talk back. If she had, there would have been quite a war between them."

"I wish I'd married and had a child," volunteered Ed. "Even if it is hard, having a baby is new life and that means something!"

"I agree. Helping Annabelle have this baby will be worth it, but the only way this pregnancy will work out well is if we all pitch in and help." Checking her supplies, she said, "Would you get me that bag of wheat flour? I'm ready for the next batch." Claire and Ed resumed their labors producing the usual assortment of good eats and friendly talk for the customers beginning to arrive.

Later in the day, Mike arrived for his weekly visit and supply of baked goods. That day, he and Ed talked about their military service, Mike having been a medic and Ed a company cook. Both claimed the right to say war is a waste of life, but admitted they had learned a lot about how to be comrades to their war buddies, which they now became to each other. Several cups of coffee later, Mike thanked them all and made a point to wave to Claire as he opened his umbrella, leaving for his doctor's appointment. Claire smiled to herself about having learned Mike had been a medic, confirming in her mind he was a good man who had helped many people. And it happened just like the Soul Self said that it would. Later, Ed talked more about what life as a company cook and a medic was like during war. Claire listened and imagined them both doing what they had to do to survive and to help others. Maybe Annabelle having this baby was a small task in comparison to war.

When Claire arrived home after work, she found Annabelle dressed and with her hair combed, watching TV with Shadow sitting beside her. Diana said it had been a good day and looked out the window just in time to see Cassie and Alexa stepping off the bus from the last day of the school year. Cassie came into the house with Alexa and looked at Annabelle and the dog with surprise. Annabelle looked back at them with curiosity. Then the two girls went into Alexa's room to sort through clothes, looking for summer shorts and t-shirts. Leaving for the kitchen, Claire and Diana talked about the schedule, but Annabelle remained in the living room, listening to the girls talk.

With a gesture of *come here*, she motioned Cassie to the floor in front of her with her hairbrush. There, Annabelle started brushing Cassie's hair and gently turning the ends into an under curl pattern. Alexa brought a pair of scissors and some hairspray and soon the curls willingly stayed in place. In the end, Cassie looked into the mirror and was pleased. She said thank you to Annabelle and then Alexa sat down in front of her, asking her to do the same for her.

Since Alexa had the same thick red hair as her Mother, Annabelle saw much of herself in the child's hair and brushed and curled it well. Alexa was also pleased with the result, which was the same style as Cassie's. For just that one moment, they were mother and daughter in a gentle way. But when Alexa offered to do Annabelle's hair, Annabelle refused and pushed her away. In the end, the three looked in the mirror and the two girls smiled. Annabelle was amazed at how happy it made the girls to have the same hairstyle. She began to see doing hair was something of value she could do for people. The girls retreated once again into Alexa's room to try on clothes for summer, but Claire noticed the event and wondered if, just maybe, doing hair could be a happy event to be repeated often that summer.

Diana and Claire had discussed the therapy schedule hanging on the refrigerator door and were working out some ideas to get Annabelle to her first physical therapy visit. Wondering if Annabelle would cooperate with the therapist, they anticipated the visit would be a challenge. Even if it went well, Annabelle would likely be given some exercises to do at home, with which Diana and Claire would have to assist. After a few minutes of discussion, Claire started a load of laundry and Diana took Cassie and Shadow home to start their evening meal. Alexa went through the TV and DVD selections and put on a program about gardening. To Alexa's surprise, Annabelle watched with interest, before falling asleep once again for a brief nap.

Anticipating Annabelle would have made a mess of the day, Thelma arrived home after work with the intention to put all things in order. However, finding that much more good had been accomplished than harm, the sometimes lioness turned into a kitten in need of her recliner. Soon Thelma joined Annabelle in the living room to rest while Claire continued preparations for supper. Indeed the duplex had turned into a place of peace where the seed of a new life had been planted by a rebellious hand. No one knew how so much good could come from such a disastrous start, but the cruel blow to Annabelle's head had, in fact, restricted much harm and allowed for some good.

After supper, Claire climbed the stairs to her apartment for her private time of writing in her journal. She had so many questions, she mentally sorted among them for the ones so important to her that she would find the answers a treasure.

Claire: How come Annabelle cannot walk or talk very well, but can do hair?

Soul Self: Ask me a question that is hard to answer. You have already observed the intention for the Highest Good implies all harm is prevented and good is made easy. Thus it is virtually impossible for Annabelle to talk back or to run away, which would be harmful, but it's very easy and enjoyable to do hair and to watch programs about positive things. In the meantime, her body is healing and the baby is developing. Indeed, much is happening that is productive of the ultimate good, love.

Claire: Yes, I sort of realized that, but thanks for confirming it for me. While I am at it, I think I have a few more questions, such as how do all of these events happen to people?

Soul Self: Why not ask the question that Einstein pondered for so long: *What is time?* When a spirit being proposes to live on the earth in physical form, a liaison is formed with all of the beings of both dimensions wanting to interact with their lifetime. Do you remember what Ed said about all plants and animals and indeed the earth itself being a family? Everything consists of conscious beings in cooperation toward a single goal.

Thus, to say one's life is fated, either ill or well, is to acknowledge all is in order by the choices of the souls engaged in the project. When an activity is needed for a good ending, such as Annabelle's release from prison, then conditions that have been in preparation for the event to go in a good way are activated at the right time. Indeed, to sit in prison for so long and never take away a single positive intention is to leave a great vacuum for good. Thus, those in Annabelle's family, both the physical and spirit ones, engage their abilities to make things happen in a way that is certain to have a good effect. All dimensions, places and things are entirely conscious and kept in place for the purpose of producing love in various ways. For a human to intend harm is merely to select the hard way versus

180

the easy way of love. As you can see, Annabelle has, up to this point, selected the hard way. Soon, she will see the easy way has its charms.

So time is like a giant conveyor belt delivering a long line of events caused to be in place in a certain order and place by conscious minds. Once one event has transpired and been enjoyed, then another comes into play and so forth.

Claire: Are you saying humans do not have free will? Are you saying they determined their fate before birth and have nothing more to do with controlling their lives?

Soul Self: Not the case! It is all far more interactive than you can understand. In one sense a plan is laid out and the events are arranged, but cooperation is voluntary. If you select one line of thought, leading to a bad end and then deselect it in favor of another one giving a better ending, then you are using free will. The result is to reshuffle the long line of events into a more favorable one for your choice.

For example, when Annabelle decides to stop being stubbornly harmful, and be a Beloved One in possession of another Beloved One for whom she cares, then the long line of negative events are canceled and new, more benign events are moved up into their place. She will do so gradually, so there will be a mix of both good and negative events, forcing her to choose good or bad over and over again. When her choice for good is solid and she does not vacillate between the good and the bad, then only good will appear.

Claire: Well, then, what is our participation? What are our choices? Really, how responsible are we for what happens to her?

Soul Self: When a being comes into life on the physical plane with a benign life plan, he or she simply follows the long line of good events delivered to them, living with amazing grace and when complete, their lifetime ends in peace. But some, like Annabelle, want to develop their human mind by strengthening the resolve for good. Your role is to support her efforts to be strong and clear in that choice. Thus the dedicated choice for good is part of the experience of being human. Do you understand?

Claire: Not quite. What if a person is strong in the choice for good and doesn't need turning events, what happens then?

Soul Self: The choice between good and bad is the task of human existence, but after that, a person exercises much creativity in forming better and better good. Think of it as evolution or even artistic creativity. Each time you paint a painting, you get better and better at merging your two minds and each painting is a different expression of beauty and truth.

But, let's get back to your life. You haven't asked the question we agreed was nearest to your own heart. Why did you choose a husband who was only barely a husband and then died, leaving you with debt? Did you choose to be harmful to yourself?

Claire: Yes, that is a good question! Tell me. I need to understand this before I make the same mistake again.

Soul Self: During your lifetime, you have been subject to cultural and social thinking that is harmful. Your life plan includes both discovering such thinking and also eliminating it.

Claire: Scott was talking about this same thing. He said I didn't exercise my rights because of misunderstandings.

Soul Self: Indeed, as a child, you were not mature enough to question your rights, but now you can and did. See how much stronger your choice will be? You can then view yourself as a fully entitled Beloved One. Also, see how prepared you will be to support Annabelle and her baby to be Beloved Ones.

Claire: I'd like them to know if they make the intention for the Highest Good, they can live a good life without pain and suffering. Whatever life plan they started with, they can change the line of events by making the right intention.

OK, now I see what you are saying. That is a good thing. I will set my intention to live my life with this understanding and try to support them in the making of good choices for themselves.

Soul Self: You do a good thing and as others do the same, it will become increasingly more difficult for harm doers to do harm on the earth and much more feasible for them to do only good.

Claire: Really, how is that?

Soul Self: That is a much longer explanation suited for a longer night. Would you like to ask another question now, such as how does the friendship with Mike continue and prosper?

Claire: Well, yes, I would like to know that. Today I learned he had been a medic in the army and I saw he was a good man, likely to do good and no harm.

Soul Self: Indeed. How could a man who had witnessed so much death and destruction while trying to save life ever contribute to harm for another? But look how he suffers from heart disease and has to visit his doctor often. Is this a sign of his intention to do himself harm? Can you give me the answer to that?

Claire: Possibly it is like Annabelle not being able to speak or walk. His illness has kept him from harm and allows him to be in places where he is loved and respected, like his doctor and our bakery. Am I right?

Soul Self: Indeed you are. The constant care of his doctor has remedied much else bothering him and delivered him to the care of the friends at the bakery. So here is your final test question for tonight. How do you know the outcome of his heart condition will be good? Is he to drop dead suddenly behind the wheel and cause many people to die, or will he recover?

Claire: Well, I think people intending good would be prevented from receiving harm, so no accident would happen to them. Their path is good and their choice is strong to do no harm. But to recover, how do you do that?

Soul Self: Very good, you passed. Congratulations. However, there is one small point you missed. Has Mike firmly decided to do only good for himself as well as for others? Might that question be the purpose of the two of you talking and being friends? Why not try talking to him about our discussion and see if he understands his next life choice is to be in love with love itself, both as it applies to himself and others? Could Mike be one of those like you, when he chooses his own good, admits true love into his suffering heart?

Claire: Oh my goodness! Now I see how we have all created the events in our lives by choice so as to be at this point in time to help each other to take the next step to love. We all need to love ourselves as well as others. Oh my goodness! This seems like a well-written play in which the characters collide on the stage in one scene to play out their plots together.

Soul Self: Precisely. William Shakespeare would be proud of you.

Claire: OK, I get it, but I need to get used to it. I want to sign off for tonight and sleep. I will think about it and see where it all leads in the next few days. Thank you so much. You have made life so much more understandable. Amazing.

With that, Claire closed her notebook and slid into bed listening to the raindrops pelting the windows and roof. She lay there beginning to be content with her life. She finally understood why and how all of the events of her life came to be. Wishing for so much more good for herself and all others, she had no idea of exactly what would happen next, but knew that it would have to be for the completion of love in all of its many expressions. The understanding she had reached released her from guilt for her past and fear for her future.

Now she clearly intended what she wanted, a good and fine life for herself and all others, confident it would be delivered by the conveyor belt of time. It was the same with all life and all people. Most importantly, she felt safe from harm and with that, love of any kind had a solid place to thrive.

Chapter 16:
Setbacks and Success

When the time came for Annabelle's physical therapy session, Diana and Claire prepared to take her to the therapy center to meet Philip Allen, her therapist. The center wasn't very far and soon Annabelle was sitting in a wheelchair, looking at a large workout room filled with equipment.

Philip began the session. "Belle, make a fist for me."

Annabelle refused, so he talked to Claire. "Have you ever seen her make a fist at home? I want to assess her arm strength."

"Her name is Annabelle. She uses her arms, but I haven't seen her make a fist."

"Belle, if you make a fist for me, you will be able to use the walking bars and begin to learn how to walk again. Please make a fist for me now."

With eyes snapping in anger, she made a fine fist and aimed it at Phillip, who was experienced enough to duck and move out of the way. "I'm sorry, but this session is ended. Bring her back when she's not combative," Philip left, making notes on a laptop.

Barely fifteen minutes after they had entered the center, they were leaving. Claire helped Annabelle into the car, saying nothing. They simply went home, where it would be for Thelma to deal with the event.

However, as soon as they arrived home, Annabelle went to the bathroom and vomited, quickly followed by diarrhea. She remained in the bathroom miserable for almost an hour. Claire tried to help by keeping her clean and comfortable. She made many trips to remove dirty clothes and to replace them with clean. After a while the sickness abated and Claire give Annabelle a shower supporting her moving around the bathroom. After the shower, Annabelle wanted to sleep, so Claire helped her into bed. Then she gathered a full load of laundry and set about washing and drying dirty clothes and towels. At last she sat down in Thelma's chair to rest.

Soon, she also was asleep, dreaming of the flowing waters of a mountain stream carrying away a kicking and screaming baby floating in a reed boat. She awoke with a start and checked on Annabelle, who was still sleeping peacefully. After a moment, she went to the kitchen to start preparations for supper, noting it was time for Alexa to return from summer camp and Thelma from work. As she peeled potatoes, she thought about the day and asked Soul Self about the events of the physical therapy and the sickness that followed.

Soul Self: From the start, Annabelle wanted nothing to do with the therapy. When the therapist made her mad by using the wrong name, taking a swing at him made her feel good, as she sensed he had little interest in putting up with her bad attitude. She matched his bad attitude with hers.

Claire: Then why did she get sick after we got home?

Soul Self: After her rage was released and she was sent home, she let go of much more rage inside and thus her digestive system responded by clearing out its passageways. It was both a consequence of her rejection of help, but also a helpful natural healing of the tensions in her body caused by anger.

Claire: Just how often is this going to happen? I don't mind helping, but I don't need too much of this kind of thing.

Soul Self: Sorry, but do you notice that no harm was done to you and in fact, you are hungry for supper. What are we having tonight?

Claire: Pot roast and mashed potatoes. But you already know that!

Soul Self: Indeed.

Claire: Wait until Thelma comes home. There will be fireworks tonight.

Soul Self: Indeed. Do you want to talk about how you felt about all of this?

Claire: Well, yes. I was shocked at what Annabelle did and angry. Then I had to clean up all of the mess. That made me madder yet. I hope that something good will come of it all.

Soul Self: Of what price is active cooperation in a course of healing? Annabelle will come back to therapy ready to do the job or she won't go at all and will sit in her wheelchair for the rest of her life. Sounds like another turning event, doesn't it?

Claire: Indeed.

Soul Self: Are the potatoes ready to boil? You'd better get the pot roast in the oven. I can hear Thelma pulling in the drive.

Claire: Thanks for the humor. I feel better.

After a description of the day, Thelma said, "She did what? I'll show her what making a fist will do for her. Where is she?"

Claire listened from the kitchen and distinctly heard the words: " And you will go back to therapy ready to do exactly what they tell you to do or you won't go at all. Then you can sit in your wheelchair in a nursing home for the rest of your life. Do you understand me?" Then there was silence. Then there was supper. Annabelle didn't say a thing and Thelma never talked about the incident again.

+*+

Later that week, Claire had another counseling session with Scott. She had thought a lot about what they had discussed in the prior sessions.

"Welcome back, Claire. I am curious, what have you been thinking about our last conversation?" started Scott.

"I talked to my friend Thelma about standing up for my rights and she said 'About time!' I guess you pointed out a good thing for me, but it makes me wonder about religion."

"Well, perhaps religion will be our topic for the day, but first let me ask if you experienced depression this week."

"I didn't have time to be depressed. I guess I still have some depression, but not as much or as often."

"Very good," said Scott. "I take your report as a measure of how well I am helping you and that means a lot to me. Do you understand?"

"Yes, you want the best for me and I appreciate it. Thank you," Claire said sincerely.

"OK, let's talk about religion today," said Scott, picking up on her thought. "Religion is all about one's relationship with God, is it not? Although religions address many issues, the way you view yourself and God is what really matters. Tell me what you think about God."

"I'm sure God is good and I am basically good, but so many bad things happen in life, I have often wondered how a good God could allow bad even for good people. Most people ask the same question, I'd guess," said Claire, interested in what Scott thought.

"People are not perfect and they do a lot of bad things. Believe me, I see it all of the time. I think God gave us free will, so therefore lots of mistakes get made. What do you think?"

"Apparently so. I can't pretend to be perfect and not make mistakes. So what's to do?"

"That's where religion can be a help. Most religions teach how to live a good life and to distinguish good from bad. But then it is up to the individual to make the commitment to do good and learn from mistakes," Scott said.

"So for me the mistake was to think I was not equal and look what it got me. Right?"

"Something like that. So where are you going to go from here?" Scott challenged.

"I don't know exactly, but I like working at the bakery and my life with Thelma and Alexa. I guess I will just continue with that and see what happens."

"Sounds like a path with no harm and lots of good! It will probably lead to more happiness." Scott made the statement absently as he was making notes, but Claire recognized the message as coming from a Soul Self intent on helping her. She smiled and said a little prayer of thanks.

Scott looked up after finishing his notes and asked, "So what else did you want to discuss?"

"I wanted to discuss more about some religious experiences that I've had," started Claire. "My husband always said I'm a mystic."

"Then tell me about being a mystic. By the way, what is the definition of a mystic?"

"My definition is when I can feel God. I have to be in a quiet, peaceful place and get my mind very quiet and still, then it comes to me when I ask for it. As a child it felt like a soft wave of warm water that lifts you up and everything is OK. Sometimes I get answers to my problems."

"OK, this sounds like what people call a religious experience. So why are these experiences so important to you?"

"Because they are happening again, only in a different way. And the questions and answers are very clear. I can write them down word for word. I keep a notebook full of them."

"Interesting. What kinds of notes are they?" Scott was not sure what was coming next.

"Well, I have to back up a bit and tell you about the little book that Thelma gave me that nobody can understand. It's called *The Long Story*, but it is a very small book. I started reading it and the mystic experiences started. I think it is much like being psychic."

"So what does the little book say?" Scott was so mesmerized he forgot to take any notes.

"It says that God is love and lives in peace and made souls to love him back. The souls all know and love each other and they live within the body of God. Then God made the universe and our solar system came into being. Souls took the life that God gave them to develop and made all kinds of life forms, including humans. So humans developed a human mind and the soul has a soul mind. The soul minds can communicate with the human mind if there is cooperation. Only fear keeps them apart. The soul is all wise and has much power over what happens to a person." Claire checked her recollection to see if she had described it clearly.

"I see, go on."

"If a person can get peaceful, and ask a question without doubt, they will establish communication and will get all of the help they need to be happy. Everybody can do it if they can get past the fears. That's as far as I've gotten," finished Claire, looking intently at Scott.

"So have you established communication?"

"Yes, at times I can do it. If I am upset, I have to calm down, but I've been keeping a notebook asking questions about how life works and my problems in particular. It has helped me a lot." Claire had let the cat out of the bag for sure. She looked at Scott to see if he would judge her harshly for what she had said, but she only saw that he was thinking about it.

"I'll have to give this some thought. It sounds something like what the Bible says, but with some differences. But it makes sense." Scott was sincerely processing the ideas. Soon he was lost in thought, looking up at the ceiling. "So what kinds of questions can a person ask?"

"Anything as long as it is for good. Souls won't give any harm."

"Suppose I ask about reducing my car payments," asked Scott with humor.

"Then you'd get good advice on what you could do to be happy about your finances. It's all about removing any barriers to being happy. In fact, that's how I stumbled across this whole thing. One night I prayed to be happy. Then it all started."

"What if I asked for all of my clients to be cured of their problems?"

"Then you would be guided on how to do that. It would take some practice, but it would be easy." Claire felt the roles between them had reversed and she was helping Scott, just as he had helped her.

"Sounds good. I'll have to try it sometime," Scott returned his attention to his notes on his computer.

Softly to herself, Claire said, "You already have."

Scott turned back to Claire and continued with the session. "So let's set a goal for this week and work toward achieving that goal. What do you think you could do to decrease depression and increase your happiness? It should be easy, like a piece of cake." Scott thought that the piece of cake idea was a good play on words, referring to her love of the bakery. The idea had just popped into his mind and he liked it.

Claire laughed a full and happy laugh. "I think that I will count my blessings this week. I know that will be a piece of cake."

"Good enough for me. Let's agree to meet next week and bring a list of your blessings and we will discuss them. Thanks for coming, I enjoyed our time together." Scott walked her to the door and said goodbye, happy to have had a good session with her.

Smiling to herself about the phrase *piece of cake* turning up again and again, Claire left for the bakery to begin her day of work. There, she found a nearly empty bread display case, so she hurried to start the day's baking. While she baked, she hummed a song and found that others joined in as they worked. Soon customers were coming in and enjoying the smell of fresh bread in the making, while bright sunshine streamed through the windows.

One customer made the suggestion Gwen open a little café so people could have breakfast and lunch, a thought that Gwen had often entertained herself. By virtue of recent improvements in income, she was beginning to research the costs, but had not made any decision as of yet. She commented that it would take a good cook with just the right skills and personality to make the special dishes her customers would want and to be able to work well with the existing staff. Her experience in small business had taught her a long time ago to develop a viable plan well before making any changes to a successful business.

As usual, Mike stopped in for his morning coffee and granola muffin. He was now part of the bakery family and always looked forward to talking to everybody, but especially Claire. Today, she came over to his table and sat down for a few minutes to talk, giving him an update on the physical therapy disaster.

"Sounds like the therapist could have handled it better, but he's right about being combative. Many patients are angry at the world in general and they can get hurt during therapy. So what happens now?"

"We don't know, but Diana said she is going to ask Annabelle to brush the dog's coat everyday to strengthen her grip and gradually get her to do more with her hands and arms. We'll see how that goes. How are you feeling today?" Claire inquired.

"Pretty good. I'm down to check ups once a month now."

"Hope you'll keep coming in."

"Wouldn't miss it," Mike smiled.

They chatted for a few more minutes, then Claire's bread needed tending and she left for the kitchen, leaving Mike to talk to another customer while finishing his coffee. On days like this, there was never a reason to regret anything and much to be happy about. Indeed Claire would have many blessings to count. And so week followed week with successes and failures, progress and setbacks, but the great conveyor belt of time continued to deliver more good than bad.

Chapter 17:
Sparks Fly

Life in the duplex was organized around Annabelle's care schedule on the refrigerator. Week after week, it dictated everything from doctor appointments, to educational DVD's and to exercises to be done at home. There were nutritional recommendations to use for meals, lessons in self-care, as well as periods of rest and entertainment. It took the efforts of four people and a dog to complete. The sixth, the patient, offered less and less resistance as the weeks went by and refrained from being combative.

In the meantime, with school closed for summer vacation, Alexa and Cassie were enjoying their usual summertime activities of swimming, bicycling, arts and crafts summer camp at the local recreation center and lots of downtime spent talking and sharing the secrets of childhood turning into adolescence. They followed the progress of Annabelle's care and her pregnancy, learning much about childbirth and childcare, a good experience for any young girl.

At the same time, Thelma continued to work at the nursing home where the stresses of poor management were beginning to take their toll. Each evening brought another story of shifting duties that meant more work with less support for the employees. Motivated solely by cost cutting and without careful planning, the thoughtless changes created a group of discouraged employees forced to use inefficient ways to run the kitchens and dining rooms resulting in less than desirable service to the clients. Despite Thelma's complaints and recommendations to managers, she had little hope of a remedy and could only be grateful things at home were better organized. Alexa recognized, through past experience and by the sound of the stories about work, Thelma was on a path to change jobs in the near future. But before that would ever happen, Thelma looked forward to the plans for the midsummer neighborhood luau, only a few weeks away.

Claire, on the other hand, loved her job and balanced her life between working at the bakery and caring for Annabelle. While the progress with Annabelle was slow, the interest between Claire and Mike was growing. The time came when Mike asked her out for lunch and she accepted.

The Café Espresso was just across the street from the bakery in an old building with a wide sidewalk and striped awning, designed to suggest the possibility Cincinnati could be like Paris in some ways. Tables and chairs were set out on the sidewalk for outdoor dining under a canopy. In good weather the two customers could sit in the sun and talk while the waiter came and went with a white apron, but no trace of a French accent. The menu was limited to a few salads and sandwiches, of average quality, but served fast so Claire could return to work for the afternoon.

Mike, at age 66, had light sandy/grey hair to match his grey/green eyes and was of medium build. Claire had been a light brown brunette when she was younger, but now at 65, had gentle highlights of grey. She wore her hair in a ponytail, which left her sparkling blue eyes as the highlight of her pleasant, introspective face. During that first lunch, Claire described her love of baking and how she had come to work at the bakery. They talked about the friends they had made there and laughed at their own jokes about themselves. They were content to spend the time in pleasant conversation, sunshine and interesting exchanges of opinions. Their topics of discussions arose from the small things of life, like the local political events, the way to make an omelet nice and soft or maybe how to find the nearest florist shop in a hurry by using a cell phone. As the lunches became a regular event, the time spent together became periods of stress-free sacredness, not to be sullied by bad news or the sharing of grief.

With time, the day came to share more of private thoughts and observations and so Claire broached the topic of her experiences with her Soul Self. She did so with confidence that Mike would accept her comments and offer no judgment or criticism. In return, he also shared his experiences of inspiration and intuitive guidance from his military and nursing careers and a short marriage ending in divorce. In fact, he had seen much during his life that would constitute miracles of prayer and healing. He was no stranger to relying on his most calm and private wisdom to make critical decisions, some of which helped to save lives when he was a nurse. And so by comparing notes, they came to the conclusion that they both had a common love of helping others and had done so most of their lives. At this point in their lives, however, they each needed to take care of themselves first. With this realization, their feelings of safety and acceptance grew stronger and even more stable, giving fertile ground for topics that could range deeper and closer to the heart. That is when it happened again.

Claire always had water with lemon and Mike ice tea with no sugar. One day, as they were having grilled ham and cheese sandwiches, they both reached for their glasses at the same moment. Their hands touched and a kind of zap or energy traveled between them. During a long pause, neither moved nor breathed.

"What was that?" Claire finally asked.

"Do you think it was static electricity?" replied Mike.

"No, it felt different and today would not be a day for static to build up. Do you remember it happened once before?" replied Claire.

"Yes, I do remember, but I didn't think anything about it."

They both thought for a minute and laughed, deciding they would have to try again to see if the spark would repeat.

"Ready, set, go!" said Mike with a smile, raising his hand in the high-five gesture. They clapped their hands together laughing. Their hands rebounded away from each other with the same feeling. "Is this a good sign?" asked Mike.

"I don't know, but apparently we're still alive and kicking. It's kind of interesting, isn't it?"

"You're like the genie in the bottle, no telling what will come next," said Mike with a smile, returning to his sandwich.

"Don't vex me, or I'll turn you into a frog," replied Claire, enjoying the humor.

"I'd have no trouble keeping you happy," said Mike between bites, pretending to be very careful about reaching for his iced tea. He noticed her look of concern about his statement, so he added, "Really!"

"So what would keep *you* happy?" asked Claire, turning serious.

Mike thought a moment and said, "Just being happy together. There's not much else in life that means anything to me except maybe helping other people. I do really enjoy that."

"I think that's what I want as well," said Claire shyly.

"Like I said. I'd have no trouble keeping you and me happy all at the same time. We want the same thing," said Mike with an "I told you so" tone.

"Yes, and we're both old enough to know how valuable happiness is," said Claire. "The first thing I ever wrote in my notebook was, 'I want to be happy.' Guess that's what you're saying, too. Yes, that sounds good. I think that'll work."

"I think so, too. Now don't touch me, I have heart problems, you know, " joked Mike. "It's almost time for you to get back to work. I'll see you tomorrow, same time, and same place. Stay happy and don't fly any kites in thunderstorms." Mike smiled as he picked up the check to pay.

But Claire did touch him on the top of his hand, just for good measure and the pleasure of doing so. Mike faked being in cardiac arrest. Both laughed until tears came down their cheeks. Then Claire walked across the street where the bakery friends were too considerate and polite to ask about the conversation, but they did give her knowing smiles and she blushed. Enough said.

That evening the family of four were sitting at the table in the duplex having supper. Recently, Annabelle had been able to use her hands and arms a bit better and was able to help herself to the butter bean casserole, fried chicken and salad. However, her words were still slurred and she could not yet put them into a sentence. That left the others to carry the conversation about the coming luau.

Thelma was proud to have hosted this annual theme party in her garage for the past ten years. It was the highlight of the summer for the neighborhood families who also enjoyed a good party. They all expected to bring a covered dish, wear Hawaiian shirts and bring some folding chairs. Thelma planned to decorate the house and garage with colored Christmas lights, wrap fake palm trees with white lights, and place dancing hula dolls and leis made from silk flowers in the garage. A CD player would provide the 1950's music of "oldies but goodies," along with the essential "Blue Hawaii" by Elvis Presley. The most important part of the whole event was everyone have a good time. This year would be no exception.

Thelma proposed that they play a game that would get everybody involved.

"How about name tag bingo?" she offered. " Each person has a bingo letter and number on their nametag and writes their initials on a big bingo card."

"Everyone already knows each other. They don't need name tags," objected Alexa.

"How about a dance competition?" returned Thelma.

"Now that has possibilities," Claire said. "What kind of dancing were you thinking about?"

"Well, we could have categories, like jitterbug, rock and roll, salsa, and ballroom dancing," proposed Thelma.

"What if people don't know those dances?" Alexa wisely queried.

"Well, then, how about line dancing? We can get a CD of line-dancing music with instructions and just play it," said Thelma with a smile.

"OK, that's good, but how about a few slow dances for couples?" protested Claire.

"Oh, this is going to be fun. There it is! The plan is to have two dance lines going and give a prize to the best one and then have slow dancing." Thelma envisioned the whole party in her mind, smiling. Annabelle reached for the dessert and knocked over her glass.

Wiping up the spilled drink, Claire said, "I was talking to Mike over lunch today and he mentioned he liked to help people. What would you think about him helping Annabelle with her exercises? He's stronger than we are and probably would keep her on track better."

"That depends on how cooperative Annabelle decides to be," said Thelma, waving her unlit cigarette and glaring at Annabelle. Thelma seemed to be watching invisible smoke curl upwards to the ceiling. Annabelle watched in envy, mentally sniffing the blissful aroma of tobacco. "Seems to me," continued Thelma, "Mike might be coming around more often. We should make the effort to know him properly. Let's invite him for supper sometime and we can talk."

Alexa bowed her head to smile, as she knew long ago Claire and Mike were going to be a couple. Annabelle had no clue about who Mike was and rolled her wheelchair into the living room to watch TV. Claire was grateful her family noticed her need to have Mike accepted and was welcoming him by inviting him to supper. Indeed, this was a good family.

"How about Friday night? I'll ask him tomorrow at lunch," concluded Claire happily.

"That would be fine," confirmed Thelma. "I think I have a roast in the freezer. We'll have mashed potatoes and gravy with green beans. Then I'll make an apple pie. I haven't had a good apple pie in a long time. Make sure he stays to sit on the porch with us afterwards and talk awhile."

With that, they washed the dishes, swept the floor, wiped the table clean and all adjourned to the front porch for the viewing of the sunset. With the warmer weather, the porch had become just as valued as any room in the house. From the vantage point of the porch, the family could enjoy the natural environment, discuss their day, entertain each other with stories and talk to passing neighbors. It was the intersection of peace and happiness. Even Annabelle liked it.

Later that night, Claire wrote in her notebook. She asked about the energy that sparked between her hand and Mike's.

Claire: Today Mike and I discussed the spark of energy that jumps between us when we touch. It feels like static electricity. Would you explain it to me? I will share your comments with Mike.

Soul Self: Indeed the little spark was an exchange of energy of the bioelectric kind. When one of a higher charge comes into contact with one of a lower charge, they equalize and a bit of energy transfers across the skin.

Claire: So you are saying that the human body has electric charges?

Soul Self: First, I must explain that you, a human body lives within a weak electro magnetic field that surrounds it, called the human aura. It is where the Soul Self supports human life energy. If you would visualize an egg, you are the yolk and I am the clear fluid in which you are suspended. The shell is the thin and permeable boundaries that come in contact with other energy eggs such as Mike's. Today, your energy shells made contact and some energy was transferred between them. It's a yolk kind of thing!

Claire: Oh, that's funny. Good yoke! I can see the analogy of the egg, but I got stuck on the idea I am suspended within you. I thought a soul was a separate thing that everyone had, but nobody knows where it is. Of course, I am relying on what religion taught me when I was a child. I never had a clear idea of what a soul is. Help me out here.

Soul Self: The Soul is not very well explained in any religion, so I will take it a bit further for your understanding. When you started reading the little book months ago, you found that God created Beloved Ones for the purpose of loving them. What you have not yet understood is that the Beloved Ones are souls that never left the body of God. We are all suspended within God and humans within the soul. It is sort of like a uterus of a mother who produces an egg and when it is fertilized, carries it, feeds it and develops it to completion. But God never delivers the offspring anywhere else but within herself. Oops, I didn't mean to imply that God has gender, but it is true God has a uterus.

Claire: Wait a minute! I thought God was in heaven, which is a very long way away and we only get there when we die, if we are good. You are saying we are already there and never left God. Wow, that is a very different way to look at things. So then you say, just as you are suspended in the amniotic fluid of God, so to speak, that I am suspended in you. That puts a whole new light on things. Let me think about that.

OK, now here is the next question: So if we are all suspended in the nurturing fluid of God, where are the earth, the stars, and the solar systems?

Soul Self: Same place.

Claire: WOW! God must be really big.

Soul Self: Indeed, and think of how very creative God is to have made all of this out of a desire to enjoy being love itself.

Claire: I can't find any objections to this because it is too far out there to even grasp, so let's go to the next question. Why does energy spark between two humans, each floating within their souls? This is either getting really weird or very profound.

Soul Self: When two people come together to interact, it is always by Soul agreement. Actually, souls are always in contact with each other, but for the sake of this conversation, let's say that your soul, me, myself and I, contacted Mike's soul to make arrangements for some good to happen for the two of you. We would set up the whole thing so it would go smoothly and give a lot of good. In this case, Mike is in the process of healing his heart condition, and you and I have great love for healing, so we proposed he be given exactly the energy that would take him to the next step of his healing. It felt like electricity, but it was a form of bio-energy we formed around the two of you.

Claire: I had no idea all of this is going on. So just for my information, suppose I gave a lot of energy to a lot of people, would I run out of energy?

Soul Self: We would just borrow some more from God since we are swimming in it.

Claire: I was going to ask if we had to give it back, but that would be foolish. If God is so big the universe is within him, he, sorry she, has plenty to give.

Soul Self: Yes, and each time we give energy away, we take more in from God, so we become more and more like God. It is really more of a gift for us than for the other.

Claire: Oh! So that explains people who can heal others. It might also include the stories from the Bible of people being healed by the laying on of hands. But to get back to my other question for today, what about Mike and me? Are we falling in love? We only today decided to just be happy together. Is that falling in love?

Soul Self: That depends on the definition of love you use to compare against your most blissful experience today. If society declares love to be one thing, but people who are truly happy find it to be something else, which one would you follow?

Claire: The people who were truly happy, of course.

Soul Self: Then look at your parents. Neither of them were perfectly beautiful people who made love ten times a day and were fascinated with each other, were they? They were ordinary people who thought they could get along and joined together to help each other be happy and raise a family. They were essentially two totally free people engaged in cooperating in the accomplishment of the same goal.

Claire: Wait a minute! Are you saying that all of the romantic love stories that are a big part of our entertainment are feeding us ideas that are not necessarily love?

Soul Self: Some are and some are not. But if you are looking for love, please realize that you are floating in it and to find someone you can get along with to do something good together is not really all that hard. There are lots of good people who enjoy working together and would like a partner either for a long time or a short time.

Claire: Oh, my goodness, now you are challenging my ideas of marriage. Where will you stop? You are changing my whole idea of reality. Please slow down and explain all of this to me.

Soul Self: Marriage is a great institution for long-term projects such as raising children and forming families, or maybe just helping each other through an entire life. As long as both parties are respected and given their freedom to be themselves and are not forced into being a copy of what the other expects, marriage is a wonderful thing. But there are also many times when two come together and don't require the marriage contract. They are free to arrange what they need.

Claire: Well, that does make some sense. I think George and I had the wrong idea when we got married. We wanted the security of a marriage and a spouse, but didn't intend to start a family, or really to do anything good. We didn't think at all. We just got married.

Soul Self: The intention to be secure together is a good intention and it would have succeeded as a marriage even without children if there had not been so much fear involved. Indeed there was some love, but far more fear.

Claire: Fear? What kind of fear?

Soul Self: You feared he would not respect your rights and you would be helpless to object and he feared he was not as good as you. Thus when he retired, he became depressed and couldn't rise out of the feeling.

Claire: Oh no! It was doomed from the start. I just can't get it right!

Soul Self: That sounds like a lot of fear, self-criticism and regret. Do you want to sign me off so you can attend to your fears?

Claire: NO! Don't leave me! I know all about the fears, I've been living with them for years. I know where they are and how they work. You are the only happiness that I've had for so long, I don't want to lose it. Please stay.

Soul Self: Stay? That's a good yoke joke. We cannot be parted because we are living within each other. I was implying that you could turn your attention from me to your human thought process. It is all your choice of where you put your attention. I am always here, always and forever.

Claire: Oh, I forgot. You said that I am the egg yolk floating in the egg. Well, if that is the case, then I don't have to go very far to find you or worry I have to be good to earn your attention. Well, I have to think a minute about that. If I can choose to give my attention to you or to my fears, then I'll have to stay focused on good and put the fears aside. This is confusing. Help me again.

Soul Self: We are back to the ground rules for communication. Since fear only exists in the human mind, you also can see how they are barriers between us. If you are willing to be peaceful with yourself and be friendly with me, seeking the highest good and nothing else, then you know where to find me and all of the information and energy I have to offer. It is your choice, but I sincerely hope you put your fears aside and continue to talk to me. I just love our relationship.

Claire: Me, too. I'm not going anywhere else. By the way, do you have a name?

Soul Self: Many, but you could call me *Sparky* or simply *Blue You* because I have the color blue in my energy field and give much of it to you.

Claire: Blue You. That's funny, sort of like "Blue Hawaii." I'm going to bed. Love you, Blue You.

Soul Self: Ditto. Blue to you, too.

And so the notebook closed again for the night and Claire pulled the covers over her head, her mind exhausted by the wrenching work of examining the basic concepts of human existence and human relationships. Much like cleaning out a closet, one has to take everything out, decide what is needed and to be kept and the rest to be discarded. Such conversations have the effect of simplifying things. Although there was much more to be learned, the first pass of clearing out the fuzzy thinking about love relationships had been accomplished. The best thing was, it left room for another person to be with her in peace and still keep freedom intact for both.

With the moon shining in a dark blue sky, the night fell quietly so all could rest before a new and more beautiful day would dawn. Since no one who had decided to be happy could expect to be happy when they were sick or greatly afraid, the Soul Selves, who were wide awake and never slept, were busily rearranging energy particles this way or that for the purpose of healing all fears and illness. Indeed it was a slow process, but it proceeded as reliably as any moon ever traversed a blue night sky, knowing that it, too, was swimming in a sea of God.

Chapter 18:
When I Fall in Love, Then What?

Plans had been made to have Mike come to the duplex for a fine roast beef dinner. But when Friday arrived, Thelma was a little late getting home from work, and so as he drove up the drive and knocked at the side door, everyone was in the midst of finalizing the meal. Claire let him in with a smile and he made himself comfortable at the kitchen table. They all started to talk.

"Mike, this is Thelma and Alexa," Claire made the introductions. "Annabelle is in the living room."

"Hi," said Thelma over her shoulder, waving her gravy spoon and not even turning to look. Alexa was more polite and came over, wiping her hands on a towel and shook his hand. Claire continued to fix a salad.

"So what's for supper?" said Mike, as if he had been a part of the family forever.

"Pot luck today is pot roast," quipped Thelma, pouring the gravy into her best antique gravy boat found at an antique flea market. "Get us some napkins from the closet."

Mike arose and got the napkins and together they all finished the preparations for the meal. Then Claire and Mike went into the living room and brought Annabelle to the table. Finally, as all were seated, Thelma sighed, tired from her efforts and finally took a good look at Mike. Actually, she looked past him so she could see out of the corner of her eye the distinct wavy lines of his energy field, the aura. Grateful she had the gift of seeing it, she had learned a long time ago the aura energy field around someone told a lot more about them than their physical appearance. She was lost in thought for a moment, but soon recovered her manners and said: " Mike, you go first, you're company."

"Me? Company? I'd rather just be friends. You did all of the work. You go first," replied Mike with a smile.

"You don't have to tell me twice," said Thelma, who helped herself to the roast, slicing big juicy chunks for everybody to spear and then spooning a mound of potatoes beside it to be covered with thick delicious gravy. Next came the green beans to be dipped in the gravy as well. Approval came in the form of the respect to eat and not to think: thus silence fell as all took their first bites of the delicious meal. The general consensus was that food in general is good and this meal, in particular, great.

Eventually, Thelma paused, sitting back in her kitchen chair like a queen on a throne, and once again eyed Mike and all of the others. She thought a general discussion starter would be best, so she said: "So how did you meet Claire?" as if she didn't already know.

Playing along, but planning some humor, Mike replied: "I had the misfortune of stopping at the bakery on my way to my doctor appointments. They fed me too much cholesterol and I got heart disease from it."

Claire smiled at the now familiar humor and rose to defend herself by saying, " Nobody forced you to eat all of those Danish."

"Sounds like you found a group of friends with good hearts," joked Thelma. "So don't blow your luck."

"Actually, it has been good luck. My doctor said that I have been doing better," Mike decided to be more sensible.

"And then some," Thelma said, letting some of her precognition slip into the conversation.

Soon, everybody was talking and joking just like they always did and the little family claimed yet another member. They discovered Mike had been a medic in the army and later a nurse, now retired. But all of the time, Mike was watching Annabelle and how she was handling her arms and hands. After a while he became convinced she would do well to exercise the large muscle groups to support the fine motor coordination. At some point, he noticed the schedule on the refrigerator door and got up to study it.

He asked a few questions and then thought aloud, "What would you think, if I got her to take some walks with me? That would get her out using her whole body and we could work on balance and coordination."

"She took a swing at the last person who tried to get her to walk. You better talk to her," replied Thelma.

"Who knows, in my condition, she may have to hold me up. We'll find a way to get along. She would be much better off to be mobile. Annabelle, what do you think?" Mike turned to Annabelle, who only shrugged.

"She's pretty stubborn," said Thelma.

"What does she like doing?" Mike asked.

"She likes doing hair," said Alexa.

"She likes cigarettes, but she's pregnant and I don't want her smoking," said Thelma, moving her ashtray.

"She does like sitting on the front porch," said Claire.

"How about dessert? Does she like dessert?" asked Mike.

"Oh, yes," they all said.

"Well, then, while you are cleaning up the dishes, I will take her for a walk down the driveway and we can bring her dessert to the front porch," proposed Mike.

"Let's give it a try!" declared Thelma, completely impressed with Mike's suggestion. She got up and walked around the kitchen, showing the beautiful apply pie to everyone, especially Annabelle.

After the meal and conversation was fully enjoyed, Claire and Alexa got up to clean the kitchen and Mike helped Annabelle's up, leading her to the door. She resisted. Thelma said to her, "Annabelle, I'll take your apple pie to the front porch if you go with Mike and get some exercise. It will help you to walk better." Annabelle relaxed.

Mike led Annabelle to the side door off of the kitchen. There, he decided the ramp was good for the wheelchair, but for this purpose, she would be better using the steps. He went down the first step and then turned around to support her as she took the same step. After the first step, she stopped, afraid. He held her hands and waited for a long time. Finally, she took another step and then another. Soon they were on the driveway. She stole a look at him. He saw it, but just stood beside her, supporting her.

They then began to walk down the driveway to the sidewalk. She proceeded to do her shuffle as she had gotten used to doing. Mike asked her to lean on his arm and lift up one foot with each step. Then he took the same step so they moved together as she leaned from side to side, taking step after step by lifting her feet. By the time they got to the sidewalk in front of the house, the steps to the front porch seemed a great challenge, so Mike called Claire and each took one arm and helped her up the three steps. As she sat in the swing, she looked relieved to be sitting. Thelma brought out a tray of plates with apple pie and forks. She put Annabelle's plate on the banister beside the swing. Annabelle would have to reach out to get it and she was likely to do so. They all sat and enjoyed the pie with secret smiles for having seen Annabelle do more today than she had done in a month. Yes, Mike would be a lot of help.

"So, Mike," started Thelma, "where'd you grow up?"

"In Iowa, on a farm," Mike picked up on the conversation. "I came to Cincinnati after Vietnam to go back to school. I was a nurse in a hospital."

"Cincinnati is a big town, but I grew up on a farm myself. I had a big family," continued Thelma.

"Me, too."

"So did your family have fights over mashed potatoes, like Thelma's," Claire saw an opportunity to embarrass Thelma a little and start some fun."

"You, too?"

"Oh, no," moaned Alexa, anticipating they would start to compare notes on growing up in big families.

"We thought you had good manners," teased Claire, knowing nothing would stop the two from comparing stories of farm family life.

"Well, we did. My parents were very strict, but my four brothers and two sisters got into a lot of trouble. We must have driven them crazy," continued Mike.

"Like what?" probed Thelma, sensing a good laugh.

"Well, when I was twelve, my brother and I tracked mud into the house on our boots. Mom laid us out for it and made us take our boots outside and wash them with the hose, then clean the floor. When Dad came home he did the same thing and Mom just gave him a kiss and a hug. So my brother and I screamed and carried on that Dad got to do it, but not us. Mom said that was different. Dad just laughed and took his boots outside."

"That's nothing," said Thelma. "We had a cow pasture next door to us and one day I collected some manure in a bucket and set it on the steps outside the back door while I went in to change clothes. When I came back, it was gone and I knew one of my brothers were up to something. That night, they put the bucket under my bedroom window so I'd have to smell it all night. I knew I had to get him back. Every Christmas, we had the Evil Elf award for whoever in the family did the worst pranks. That year, I made sure he got it. He had to recite his list of pranks and beg forgiveness in front of the whole family."

"So what were you going to do with the bucket of manure before your brother got it?" asked Claire, sure that Thelma would have had something in mind.

"Why put in his boots, of course." Everyone gasped, as they comprehended her own Evil Elf duplicity. Then they all laughed.

Recognizing no one could top a story Thelma might tell, they turned the conversation to a variety of topics like how to make perfect pie crust, how fun it was to grow up in the fifties and sixties, who knows who in the neighborhood, stories from the nursing home, silly things done at the last luau and, of course, the invitation to Mike to attend the coming party. Then they asked Alexa if she and Cassie were going to invite some friends and got a resounding "no." Everyone laughed.

After a while, Alexa and Claire asked Mike if they could have a walk as well and the three headed down the sidewalk, chatting about Alexa's friends, school and her ambition to be an archeologist. Thelma got Annabelle up out of the swing and took her inside to give her a shower and prepare for bed. One would think that during intimate moments between mother and daughter much sharing would take place, but kindness between them was still difficult.

Truthfully, Thelma was not sure just how much Annabelle understood of what was said to her. The damage of the blow to her head was not fully defined and the situation changed from week to week. Fortunately, she was becoming more functional in the simple processes of life. Thelma did, however, notice Annabelle's growing pregnancy, which brought a worried shudder to Thelma's heart.

With Annabelle in bed, Thelma returned to the porch for her last cigarette for the day, but instead, she had another piece of pie waiting for the walkers to return. As she looked upward, she slipped into psychic thought and she mused about many things on her mind just as Claire so often did in her notebook. During such times, Thelma forgot about all of her problems and enjoyed much contentment. Like Claire, this awareness of her Soul Self was more precious than anything else in life and much to be savored.

Within an hour, the three walkers returned and Mike thanked them for the dinner and evening. They thanked him for his help with Annabelle, inviting him to come often. Such were the simple friendly gifts that make for a neighborly visit, and Mike left well satisfied with the time that was had. The three housemates agreed he would do just fine for them all as a friend and for Claire's gentleman friend in particular.

After Alexa went into the house to go to bed, Claire and Thelma talked on the porch.

Thelma offered her opinion. " I like Mike. He won't hurt you."

Claire appreciated the approval and said, "I do, too, but I don't necessarily want to be more than friends for a while. I still feel exhausted with my life. I can't handle much else."

"I know what you mean."

"I am beginning to think falling in love isn't what it's all about. It's more about friendship and companionship," Claire offered some of the profound thoughts from her notes.

"That would surely be easier than falling in and out of love over and over again," replied Thelma ruefully.

"Do you ever want to have another relationship with a man?" Claire probed.

Thelma replied quickly, "Not really. There are times when I feel lonely or want someone paying attention to me, but it all comes with so much baggage, I just can't stomach it."

"Soul Self was talking about fear. When a relationship is founded on fear, it never goes right, unless there's a lot of love to overcome it. What do you think?

"I'm not afraid of anything. Maybe that's why I never remarried. Who would want me?" Thelma laughed.

"I've been afraid of everything and everybody all of my life."

Thelma started in a new direction: "You know he's not going to have heart problems anymore, don't you?"

"You think so? I *so* hope so. Wait a minute. Soul Self was saying that I am giving Mike blue energy for his healing. Is that what you are talking about?"

"Yeah, that's it."

"Can you see the blue energy?"

"Sometimes."

"What do think about me and Mike?"

Going into her psychic thoughts, Thelma replied, "Many happy days and much to do that is good. What do you see for Annabelle?"

Claire did the same as Thelma and replied, "Soul Self says that she will recover many of her abilities, but never be able to speak the ugly words she used to say. She will be a strong mother just like you. The baby will be fine, but will not have her stubbornness. This child will charm her into learning a thing or two." (Laughing)

"I thought so, but thanks. What do you think I should do about my job?" asked Thelma, meaning what did Soul Self think.

"Soul Self says to be patient and things will be worked out in time. Don't make any sudden decisions until a new opportunity is available."

"Thanks. It sure is a lovely evening. Friendship is such a gift. You know that I love you."

"Ditto. I don't know very many people who can speak Soul Self to me. Do you ever tell other people about it?"

"Not unless they ask. It's something that you have to want to know," Thelma concluded.

"Yes, it is."

They sat and chatted, traveling through many topics under the rising moon and twinkling stars until both were tired and they retreated to bed.

The conversation between Claire and Thelma had been a brief one, but it was significant. They had both created a quiet and peaceful moment in which to hear their Soul Selves and share the good and wise Soul information for each other. It doesn't get much better than that between two people. Once started, these types of friendships tend to create a strong feeling of love and security because no harm is ever done and much good given. No further expectations are needed and neither threatens the freedom or character of the other because neither is afraid of anything. The significance of their conversation was trust. It was the trust that gave everyone a good night's sleep and confidence to rise in the morning and continue on the life path they had set before themselves.

As Claire climbed the stairs to her apartment, she was unaware what would come during the eagerly anticipated luau that would send sparks across many more barriers of comprehension. After all, when one knocks on the door to everlasting peace, love is sure to answer. And like pink flamingoes, love is free to take flight in a blur of pink wings traveling to places yet unknowable.

Chapter 19:
A Magical Night

The preparation for the luau was not elaborate, but it did require certain things be brought from storage and made available. First of all, Mike, who had never been to a luau, but had been in Hawaii, needed to find an old Hawaiian shirt he thought he still had somewhere in his attic. It took a day and a half of sorting through old things and old thoughts to find it, but he did. Its design was of the old style with pale colors and tall palm trees lining golden beaches. He tried it on and fortunately it fit. With just a good laundering and a pair of slacks, he was ready for the party.

Claire and Alexa had agreed to go back to the Goodwill store and search for something tropical and party frilly for themselves and Annabelle. They didn't have much hope that she would participate, but they wanted to make the effort. After a sincere search, Claire found something for herself, a frilly pink blouse with pearl buttons down the front and some sparkly pins including the ultimate find of all times, pink flamingo earrings to give to Thelma as a surprise. Then she made the outfit complete with a flowy skirt of pale lavender, with blue and pink flowers.

It was uncharacteristic for Alexa to wear a dress, however, since none of her friends except for Cassie were coming to see their humiliation doing "old people" dancing, she allowed that a frilly dress with an elastic waist would be OK. The fabric had a dark green background with many flowers and flowing colors running riot from top to bottom.

For Annabelle, they debated a long time. Unsure she would even attend or wear what they bought, they nevertheless wanted to find something acceptable to her. In recent years, Annabelle's only fashion choice had been black t-shirts with weird symbols on them, so the shoppers wanted something simple but pretty, for she *was* pretty. Considering her dark auburn hair and dark eyes, they decided on a dark red satin top, long enough to give some flow and cover her emerging baby bump. It would go with whatever pants she was comfortable wearing and featured a fabric belt. All of the purchases together were about $20 and so they considered the shopping trip a success.

Thelma, had already found her dress earlier in the year, only needed to find matching leis and some obscenely high heels to wear on her aching feet. Her other concerns rested with finding the old hula hoops she had stored somewhere, trying out the lighted palm trees to be sure all of the lights worked and locating the line dancing CD. The rest of the planning consisted of setting up food and drink and the Tiki bar in the garage, all of which Mike had volunteered to help her with on the morning of the party.

When the Saturday morning of the luau arrived, which was also Fourth of July, there was much to be done by 7 in the evening, when guests would arrive. Fortunately, Mike arrived about 8 a.m., in time for a hearty duplex breakfast and a long list of things to be done. He and Thelma then went out to the garage and began moving things around, sweeping and laying extension cords. The blow-up baby swimming pool was filled with water and yellow rubber ducks bobbing, so anyone moving their folding chairs to its edge could put their bare feet in the water and talk while moving the ducks around.

The Tiki bar was a bit unsteady, but bracing with a few bits of hardware worked pretty well, giving it a beachcomber look straight out of vintage *Gilligan's Island*. In addition, stacked crates were made available to store the pop, beer and wine people would bring for the evening's enjoyment. Above the bar were a few signs like: "Shop until you drop, drink until you forget," "Friends don't let friends do dumb stuff alone, they do it together," "What would Jimmy Buffet do?" and the totally hilarious, "Does doing the hula make my butt look good?" These signs were lit with carefully wired Christmas lights that twinkled. In fact, the whole ceiling of the garage was a network of crisscrossing multicolored lights shining down on folding tables covered with colored tablecloths. On the tables were vases of flowers Alfred had brought, making the aroma of roses quite romantic. No one could miss the intention of the party.

Thelma also wanted lights put up on the front porch. She had purchased dozens of boxes of Christmas lights at the last year end sale. Mike, being a good friend and family member already, hung the lights from the ceiling of the porch. He also lined up the pink flamingoes along the edge of the walkway, stringing lights between them, so all would see them and no one would trip. Actually the porch colored lights would, by popular demand, stay for quite a long time as they seemed to invite company to come and talk awhile during the long hot evenings. It was a successful innovation Mike helped to create.

While all of this was being attended to, Claire was preparing the food and Alexa was trying the red satin top on Annabelle and getting her hair styled. Alexa would have had no way of knowing, except by Soul inspiration, but the red top reminded Annabelle of a red dress Thelma had bought for her when she was a child. Annabelle had always loved that dress and so it was by Soul-to-Soul cooperation that Annabelle slipped on the top and smiled. Surprised and pleased that Annabelle liked the red top, Alexa sighed in relief knowing she had guessed right. She was also surprised Annabelle let her do her hair. In the end, Annabelle would look pretty and although she would probably just sit most of the evening, she would be a part of the happy party without disrupting it. Good enough for now, Alexa thought.

After that, Alexa left to go to Cassie's house to see what her friend had selected to wear and ask if she wanted Annabelle to do her hair as well. There, she found Cassie's mother ironing the Hawaiian clothes that she and her husband Robert always wore to the luau. Later she would prepare a covered dish of baked spaghetti with meatballs as a contribution to the food. Robert was mowing the yard, but promised to shower and dress in time for the party. In fact, much of the neighborhood was thinking about the party and making preparations.

After the decorations met with Thelma's approval, she sat with an unlit cigarette and thought about the many years of giving this party and how much had changed each year. This year was special in that Annabelle had returned home and had the prospect of being a mother. Also, this was the first year Claire was living with them and what a blessing that had been. Then there was Mike, who became a member of the family so easily and quickly and was so much help. She had much to be grateful for and so she lit her cigarette and let a long puff of smoke stream upward with a prayer of thankfulness for her life, her family and the constant inflow of good each day. On the other hand, there was the Evil Elf award. Who would get it this year? She smiled.

She put out the cigarette and went into the kitchen to check on the food preparations, which needed no checking at all. Soon she had convinced herself she might be allowed a rest in her chair. Mike and Claire sat on the front porch, resting and talking. After about an hour, Claire laid her head on his shoulder and dozed a bit. Mike smiled at being the strong shoulder once again because, since his heart problems had occurred, he had felt his strength was waning. Living with the possibly he might have a fatal heart attack at any moment had eroded his confidence in his manly strength. Now with the family needing his help and wanting him to be part of their lives, he felt a new path in life opening up for him and he liked it very much.

He particularly liked Claire with her deep wisdom and curious, inventive mind. But it was the whole experience, which impressed him with how little it takes to turn a lonely life with a sad end into a happy one. It had started with the friendships at the bakery, then the acceptance of the family at the duplex and including him into the project of getting Annabelle functional in preparation for her baby. It all worked together to give him a good purpose. He actually felt like a family man of sorts with all of the duties and pride it entailed. He sighed deeply with gratitude and considered it all to be a blessing to be treasured, protected and nurtured. He was the man who wanted to do it and he silently wished that his heart would be healed so he could do so for a good long time.

Finally, evening came. As Cassie and Alexa were sitting on the floor so Annabelle could do Cassie's hair, they talked about how embarrassing it was to them to be associated with such a corny and old-fashioned thing as a luau. What would their friends think? Would they ever live it down if anyone found out? Then they looked out the window at the gaily-decorated garage and thought better of catering to their peer expectations.

Cassie commented, "Our parents love us and made all of this happen for the whole neighborhood. It doesn't matter if it is old-fashioned. They are old and that's OK."

Alexa laughed and agreed, " Yes, I'd rather be here than anywhere else. So let anyone come and make fun of us. We'll just laugh."

And laugh they did with wide acceptance of themselves as children, not realizing that, at the same time, they were accepting themselves as future old people. They finished their makeup and getting Annabelle dressed. They wondered if they should move the wheel chair outside so that Annabelle could sit and move around on the driveway without danger of falling, but Annabelle shook her head no. Mike helped her walk out the door and down the steps to sit in a folding chair near the food and drink.

Between 7 and 8 p.m. people began to arrive with their covered dishes and drinks. Friends greeted friends, new neighbors were introduced and everyone quickly felt at home. Despite living in a close-knit neighborhood, everyone seemed to have news to share. The Clarks shared photos of their new grandchild. Earl Land had a new job and Andrew Goebel had been promoted in the spring. In one corner of the yard, several men talked about the best features of this year's new truck models and the younger children ran around, trying to catch fireflies. Mothers admired how their children were growing up, but also how long it had been since they had time for going out with their husbands.

Thelma started the music and the party grew and expanded as more people arrived with good food and drink. Soon the spirits of the neighbors rose to those of a really good party. The line-dancing contest seemed to take everyone by complete surprise, but once Thelma grabbed a few hands and started dancing the moves, more followed. Each tried to follow the directions, some succeeding and some not so much. Eventually, the activity took on the character of a not-too-organized kick line. To select a prize would have been presumptuous, so Thelma just kept playing more records of familiar oldies and singing along with great gusto.

That was how couples spread out over the driveway, dancing the ever popular, but vintage Twist and Mashed Potato, and only a few did more recent dances. Diana and Robert laughed and gyrated to music from when they first met, which led them to recalling many good memories. Gradually, the faster dances settled into mostly slow dances. Seizing the opportunity, Mike took Annabelle's hand and asked her to stand. He held her in a soft dance position and she rested on his strength and moved to the music just as they had worked together when she took her first steps with him. They made it through one song and she tired quickly, but Mike had made the point of treating her as a beautiful woman, due respect and kindness. While neither of them spoke of it, the impact was never forgotten because she had never been treated so well by any man. Mike escorted her back to her chair and brought her some punch. For a while, he stood beside her chatting with people and they with him and Annabelle. She learned the neighbors all knew of her situation and were supportive of her and her pregnancy. As she had often made fun of these neighbors, but they never of her, it was something to think about.

Alfred stood on the sidelines for a while, but then asked Alexa to teach him some of the new dances. Alexa looked him over and decided on a simple dance that was not too athletic and took his hand to lead him through the moves. Alfred loved it and soon Cassie came over and the three of them danced together round and round. When Alfred needed to sit down and rest, they got him some punch and sat him down beside a woman who was a widow in the neighborhood. Her name was Matilda. Although they knew of each other, they had not been formally introduced. Always the gentleman, Alfred started the conversation.

"May I introduce myself? My name is Alfred."

"My name is Matilda and I live a block over. I've seen you around. My husband and I built the house I still live in, even though he died years ago," said the lovely, mature Mathilda.

"What a coincidence. My wife and I built the house next door and when she died I stayed on as well," replied Alfred.

"Oh, we live in a world of memories, don't we?" started Mathilda. "Isn't it good to have a party and see the young people and how they do things?"

Impressed with her good-natured comments, Alfred asked, "So, do you have a garden?"

"I used to have a vegetable garden, but these days it's too much work for me. But I can't give up on flowers. I just love day lilies and I collect as many varieties as I can afford."

"My wife's favorites were roses and my backyard is filled with many different varieties of rose bushes. Would you like to see them? I'll turn on my yard lights," offered Alfred, as he rose and offered his arm.

Mathilda liked his good manners and the topic of flowers enticed her still more. The two walked over to Alfred's yard and went through the garden gate.

Alfred had long ago laid out excellent paths, so the rose tour was easy and pleasant. But it wasn't quick. The two gardeners talked a long time about soil, watering, and cultivation of varieties of scents and colors. Of course, they were not in competition, but Mathilda insisted that Alfred visit her garden the next day to see what a real garden was like. Being the gentleman, he would do so, but for this moment, he had more appreciation for the woman who tended the flowers. When Alexa returned with more punch, she wondered where the two had gone. As Cassie arrived, wondering the same thing, the girls looked at each other and suddenly laughed, "You don't think so, do you?"

This prompted them to look around at all of the "old people." Diana and Robert were slow dancing gracefully, kissing and talking. Other people were sitting in chairs, talking and chatting as old friends do. A circle of children and men sat around the inflatable swimming pool with their shoes off, racing rubber ducks and making as much splash as possible. Finally, the girls spotted Claire and Mike slow dancing.

It had all started with a bit of a joke, of course. Mike came up behind Claire and unexpectedly tapped her on the shoulder, giving her a start. As she turned, he caught her in his arms and walked her out to a clear spot on the driveway dance floor. They came together gently, holding hands. Then Mike encircled his left hand around her waist and she rested hers on his shoulder in the traditional style. The music propelled them forward in a good rhythm and their bodies adjusted to each other as they began the gentle swaying together that makes slow dancing so easy. Neither talked very much, but they both enjoyed the music and being close. Slowly the crowd around them seemed to disappear and only the two of them were present under the deep purple sky sporting a bright full moon. Things seemed to be in slow motion and each note of the songs and move of their bodies was intensely enjoyable.

Mike started to hum the melody of the music and Claire liked the sound of his deep voice. She prayed fervently that his heart would be completely healed because being this near to him seemed to her, at that moment, to be just wonderful. Mike was also thinking, but his thoughts were about the music, the sky and the stars. He was so glad it was an outdoor party. *How much better than being in a stuffy room,* he declared to himself. He thought about the many nights he had looked at the sky when he was a boy and later as a medic in the war. His memories attested to the fact that when all hope was lost, he could look at the sky, which was still there in all of its peaceful beauty, and find hope. In this case it was gratitude.

He felt Claire in his arms cuddled against his chest and wanted so much to protect her from all worry and harm. He knew he could not always do so and, more importantly, she could do that herself. Better, he thought, to cherish the time they had together and keep their promise to each other to be happy whenever they were together. With that, he gave her a gentle squeeze, drawing her closer to him and she yielded.

Slowly, they became one, in contentment and appreciation of each other. Mike turned his face to her and paused as if asking if he could kiss her and she smiled. Thus, they kissed for the first time, a long, warm, good kiss. The kiss was partly to explore each other and the feeling of them being together, but also partly to give expression to the deeper feelings that were rising. At that precise moment, the town's Fourth of July fireworks started and great clouds of sparkling lights filled the sky, booming and popping in profusion. They both looked up and then laughed at the humor of a first kiss accompanied by fireworks. They squeezed each other even more closely and stood side by side watching the light show in the sky, still swaying with the music. Others joined them as the next record began to play and all sang together the words to "Blue Hawaii."

The fireworks lasted another half hour, the music for another hour and a half, and the memories for yet another year. Most couples left holding hands, and friends walked side by side. Alfred walked Mathilda home and would never confess to having received a peck on the cheek, although he did walk with a spring in his step he had begun to think would never again be there.

The food was taken into the house, but otherwise, the lights were turned off and the garage door lowered. The front porch festive lights were left on all night and Claire and Mike sat there for a long time talking, hugging and kissing. They felt young again with the feeling of being together. Leaving well after 1 a.m., Mike was sure they would be together in so many ways, and with so many things to savor, he wanted all such moments to come in their own perfect time.

Claire had the same sense. Later as she slipped into her comfortable bed, in her safe and loving home with her accepting and supporting family, she thought about her growing love with Mike. How could so much happiness have happened in just a few months? Something very big and important had happened and with all of the notes in her notebook, she could trace the steps she had taken to this precious moment. At that moment, Claire saw clearly and would later record in her notebook a single prodigious thought. "Once the door of peace is pushed open, love is sure to say, 'Welcome to yourself. You are never in search of love. You *are* Love Itself, a Beloved One, living within the Soul of Love and swimming in a sea of God. Everyone is.'"

+

To read more about the Soul Self and the lives of those who discover they are Beloved Ones, watch for additional books in the *Soul Self* series. For more about the author's notebook of

230

conversations with Soul Self, search for the series *The Book of the Highest Good* on Amazon.com as described on the author page for Joyce McCartney. Additional information is available on: www.souloflovebyjoycemccartney.com.